Check out more popular titles from
SIMON PULSE

The Private series
By Kate Brian

The Seven Deadly Sins series
By Robin Wasserman

Go Figure
By Jo Edwards

The Social Climber's Guide to High School
By Robyn Schneider

Read My Lips

TERI BROWN

SIMON PULSE
New York London Toronto Sydney

SIMON PULSE

An imprint of Simon & Schuster Children's Publishing Division
1230 Avenue of the Americas, New York, NY 10020
Copyright © 2008 by Teri Brown
All rights reserved, including the right of reproduction
in whole or in part in any form.
SIMON PULSE and colophon are registered
trademarks of Simon & Schuster, Inc.
Designed by Jessica Sonkin
The text of this book was set in Fairfield LH.
Manufactured in the United States of America
First Simon Pulse edition June 2008
2 4 6 8 10 9 7 5 3 1
Library of Congress Control Number 2007941328
ISBN-13: 978-1-4169-5868-0
ISBN-10: 1-4169-5868-1

This book is lovingly dedicated to
my beloved friend, mentor, and sensei,
Judy Brown
4/29/40–5/13/04

Supporter of kitties,
the Alexander Graham Bell Association,
and deaf children everywhere

You are deeply missed, Crusader Rabbit.

ACKNOWLEDGMENTS

So many wonderful people helped and supported me while I wrote this book. Jenny Bent, you put the "super" in "super-agent." Caroline Abbey, amazing editor, thank you for your unwavering belief in Serena and her world. Holly Root—you rock! Special thanks to grammar queen and whip master Kerensa Brougham. Thanks to Brook Taylor for not selling your first book until after mine sold! I also want to give a shout-out to Dawn Groszek and Pamela Kopfler, critique partners extraordinaire, and Alesia Holiday and all the teen-lit authors for their advice and support.

Huge hugs to my best friend, Ann Friedrick, who always believed in me.

All my love and gratitude goes to my husband, Alan, the silly man in the red sheet. You are the ultimate dream maker.

And thanks especially to my incredible kids, Ethan and Megan, for showing me how awesome teens can be. What an amazing journey we've had. Mama loves you.

One

What the heck?

I stared at the small person waving her arms like a referee.

A quick look at my schedule confirmed that this was indeed American history taught by Ms. Fisher. So who was the little umpire? The teacher? I glanced at the other students for help, but their open mouths and blank faces mirrored my own confusion. It must be Ms. Fisher.

The woman flashed me an encouraging smile and again waved her hands in a wild arc. What was she doing? Swatting a fly? Modern dance?

The answer slammed into my stomach like a stray curveball, and a mortifying heat flooded my cheeks.

If the teacher had bothered to read the bloody file, she'd have known better.

Another quick look at the class showed they were

snickering. I'd rather have them laugh with me than at me. I dropped my backpack and winked at the other kids. Letting my arms and fingers fly, I waved them around in an arc and slapped them together a couple times, mimicking the teacher perfectly. Then I looked at her expectantly.

The teacher frowned. She leaned forward and started to wave her arms about again.

I finally reached out and grabbed her hands. "I don't know sign language," I said, though the teacher's efforts hardly resembled the sign I'd learned, and forgotten, as a child. "I just talk. It's easier."

The class laughed. The teacher pulled her hands out of mine and flushed a dull brick red. "My apologies. I just assumed you'd know sign."

Recovering quickly, she then put her hand on my shoulder and faced the class. "Class, this is Serena Nelson and she moved here from Portland," she said, raising her voice. "She's deaf, so you'll have to look at her when you speak so she can read your lips. Though, from what I understand, you can hear some through your hearing aids, correct?"

I nodded. My turn to be mortified. Why did teachers always have to introduce me as the deaf girl? That was the thing about teachers. Their ability to humiliate was far superior to our ability to make them nuts.

The teacher beamed. "Isn't technology wonderful?"

Released, I snatched up my backpack and slunk over to the desk Ms. Fisher indicated. At least she'd placed me at the front of the class so I could see her face better. I ignored the curious stares. So much for slipping in unnoticed.

I whisked a covert glance around the room. Because the 'rents had moved me to the ends of the earth, I wanted to check out what kind of kids I'd be dealing with. Like being in tenth grade wasn't bad enough. Doing it in a new school was torture.

These kids looked exactly like the ones in my first two classes. I sighed. Not a skater or punk in sight. Most of the guys wore jeans and T-shirts. A little less baggy here than in the city, but typical guy wear. The girls resembled cookie cutouts. Expensive, trendy cookies. Designer jeans. Thin little Ts layered like pastel flower petals. Etnies or Nikes on their feet. I felt as if I'd wandered into Prepsville instead of a normal high school.

I glanced at my own clothes, chosen for comfort and invisibility. Vans. Dark jeans. Dark hoodie. Practically a uniform at the old school. Here I felt as invisible as a punked-out unicorn.

I noticed a guy in the corner staring at me, his eyes dark and unwavering. Unlike the other guys, he wore a plaid shirt with his jeans and black army boots instead of tennis shoes. I met his gaze and almost flinched at the electrical current that leaped between us. *Yowza!* What the hell was that? Turning away, I tried to focus on the teacher writing on the chalkboard, but my eyes flew back to the guy, who flashed me a slow, lazy grin. I returned the smile and ducked my head.

What was that about? It wasn't like me to be embarrassed around a guy. Guys were easy. First you teased 'em like they had a chance to get in your pants. Then you showed them up on the skateboard, and that turned them into normal people. Like friends. Friends you had to be careful around in case they tried to grab a handful when you weren't looking, but friends nonetheless. Better than being alone.

I looked back over at the guy sitting there all casual, as if he hadn't just burned me with a thousand-watt smile.

I tried to concentrate on what the teacher was saying but couldn't focus. The teachers were supposed to give me notes of all the lectures, so with those and the textbooks, I should be able to keep up. Hopefully. In my old school I had an actual captioner. She was an older woman whose rapid typing kept me informed of everything said in the classroom. Sometimes she'd actually give me the answers.

I opened my history book to the page the teacher had instructed and started on the assignment, though I'd rather have had my fingernails yanked out one by one. History sucked. So did English, creative writing, and any other effing class that depended on language to teach. Math was my thing. Numbers lined up and marched in nice, orderly rows, while slippery words could mean a million things.

I looked at my watch. Twenty minutes to go. Next came lunch. Maybe I could hang out at the library. Check out their manga collection. Disappear for a bit. Relax.

At my old school, lunch was for sneaking a cigarette and

doing a little skating with the guys. Randy, Greg, and Chaz were the closest things I had to friends. I missed them.

I jabbed my pencil into my notebook. I wouldn't be here at all if my parents hadn't decided to move closer to family. And where was that precious family we'd moved five hundred miles to be close to? On vacation! Some family. I liked my aunt and uncle okay, but they'd had a couple of babies. Now I'd have snotnosed little cousins to deal with. They'd probably want me to babysit all the time. Plus they'd taken in a teenage boy—probably some loser. Aunt Shirley has a serious save-the-world complex.

A note flew over my shoulder and landed onto the desk. What the hell? I picked it up and opened it.

You want to sit with me at lunch?

My stomach clenched. I turned to look at the girl sitting behind me. Soft gold hair all flipped up at the ends. Glowing skin. Lips curving into a sweet smile showing orthodontist-perfect teeth.

I turned back to the note, remembering all the do-gooders in my life who'd treated me like a charity case but would never admit it.

I added a line to the note. *Why? U feel sorry for me?*

I folded the note before flipping it back over my shoulder. I waited.

It came sailing back a moment later.

Well . . . yeah.

I laughed out loud before clapping a hand over my mouth.

The teacher glanced up but didn't say anything.

Okay. Cool, I wrote and sent the note back. That was a first. Girls like that usually don't have a sense of humor.

A tap on my shoulder a few minutes later told me the bell must have rung. If I'm listening, I can usually hear it, but I can miss a bell if I'm concentrating on something else. I shoved my books into my backpack and turned to the girl waiting behind me.

"My name is Rachel."

Not even my high-powered hearing aids could pick up Rachel's soft voice. At least she wasn't yelling like some people did.

"If you lower the tone of your voice and talk a bit louder, I could probably hear you better," I told her as we headed out of the classroom for the cafeteria.

Another girl from history class sidled up to us. Her eyes barely flickered over me as Rachel introduced us. The girl, whose name was Kayla, gave me a tight smile.

"Rach, can I talk to you? Alone?"

Rachel frowned and glanced at me.

"Go ahead, I'll wait."

She walked a little bit away from me and Kayla grabbed her arm. They were both blondes, but Rachel had the princess thing going while Kayla looked like a streaky-blond beach bimbo.

"Do you think this is a good idea?" I read Kayla's lips as easily as if she had been talking to me.

"What?" Rachel wrinkled her nose like a baffled child. I pretended to study some antismoking posters on the wall. Then I looked back and concentrated on their lips.

Kayla rolled her eyes. "Taking a deaf chick to lunch this close to *you know what. They're* making out the lists this week."

Rachel shrugged. "Sorry, done deal. I'm just being nice. They can't kick me out because of that."

Kayla didn't look convinced, but Rachel had already turned away and was heading back to me.

I had no idea what they were talking about. Kicked out of what? Who cared? I was both thankful that Rachel was as nice as she seemed and pissed off by it. I hated people feeling sorry for me.

"You ready?" she asked.

Kayla had already headed down the hall.

I nodded and we fell in step toward the cafeteria.

Rachel said something, but she was facing straight ahead and I couldn't catch it.

I cringed. Training new people sucked. Which is why I usually didn't bother. "What?" The worst four-letter word in the English language.

Rachel turned her head so I could read her lips. "I said, how can you be deaf and have hearing aids?"

I sighed. Why did people always want to know so much? Couldn't they get that I'd rather not discuss it?

"Without my hearing aids I can't hear anything. With

them I can hear some things. Certain voices and sounds."

"So you read lips to hear what's going on?"

I smiled. "Yeah, you could put it that way." We walked a little bit while I tried to think of something to say. What did you talk about with a girl like Rachel? "So what was Kayla worried about you getting kicked out of?"

Oops. Wrong subject. Rachel's eyes widened and her footsteps faltered. "How did you. . . ? Oh. The lipreading thing. Um, nothing really . . . just a school thing."

Something wasn't right. Rachel's eyes slid away from mine and her shoulders tensed up. Definitely not a girl who liked lying, and she was *so* lying. Reading body language was a specialty of mine. Came with trying to figure out what people meant all the time. So why the need to lie?

The scents of overboiled hot dogs and Thousand Island dressing assaulted me as we entered the cafeteria. We paid the lunch lady and I balanced my tray in one hand and backpack in the other. "Where do you sit?"

Rachel gestured. "Over here." She led me to a table next to the vending machines. "It's near the door and the drinks."

My heart plunged. One sweeping glance around the table confirmed that these were natural A-listers, so pink and polished they might have leaped from the pages of *Seventeen* or *Teen Vogue*. Magazines I wouldn't be caught dead with, by the way. I would've given anything to be hanging out behind my old school with the guys right now.

I dumped my backpack under the bench and set my tray on the table while Rachel introduced me. She gave out their names and class like serial numbers. Twins Kelly and Kayla, sophomores. Patrice, junior. Sonar, junior. *Sonar?* What misguided soul would name their kid Sonar? And why on earth was Rachel telling me what grade they were in? Like it mattered or something.

All the girls were impossibly shiny and put together. They murmured a disinterested greeting and returned to their conversations. I sat, torn between disappointment that they didn't include me and relief. Screw it. Better than sitting alone.

I didn't try to follow the conversations going on around me and discreetly turned my hearing aids down. Too many voices jumbled together into an annoying buzz. Instead I picked at my food and pretended to be incredibly interested in the rest of the cafeteria. It could have been any cafeteria in any school in America. Totally generic. Tons of windows, graffiti-scarred tables, and an unending expanse of concrete. The food wasn't bad, though. I took a bite of my chili dog and looked around again. There had to be some skaters or punks around here somewhere, right? Or maybe this was like that movie, *The Stepford Wives*, only with ridiculously perfect robot teens.

My attention focused on two adults standing next to a door with a TEACHERS ONLY sign on it. The woman's crossed arms and set expression looked grim. The man held his arms stiffly by his sides and his eyes scanned the students. They stopped talking whenever a teacher came to or went from the door.

I focused on their lips out of habit. The woman spoke clearly, her words enunciated and crisp. I caught almost everything. "I told you not to call me at home," she said. "What if Rex had answered? Only call my cell."

"But I needed . . . I love you so . . ." the man answered. His lips were half hidden by his mustache, which made it hard to read his words. But even from a distance I could see the pleading in his eyes.

A tap on my shoulder jolted me from the soap-opera scene. Rachel indicated a dark-haired girl—I remembered her name as Patrice—at the end of the table.

Patrice nodded her head toward the teachers. "That's Mrs. Weber, the music teacher, and Mr. Bernard, the PE teacher." She leaned forward, her sleek hair falling over her shoulders with a glossy swing. "Everyone thinks they're having an affair."

"They are," I said without thinking.

Down the row, heads swiveled toward me. The girls who'd ignored me moments before now stared with their mouths open.

I liked that.

Patrice's eyes narrowed. "How do you know? You just got here."

I shrugged. "I can see their words."

Everyone turned to look at the couple, then back at me.
"But how do you know?" Patrice demanded.

Rachel slammed her hand onto the table. "Oh my God,
you're reading their lips." She paused. "I'm right, aren't I?"

Excitement lit up Patrice's green eyes like a Christmas
tree. "You can read lips? Even from across the room?"

A field trip I'd taken years before flickered through my
mind. It was before I was mainstreamed, when I was still
going to the deaf school. We took a bus downtown and
practiced reading lips. The teacher hadn't believed me when
I told her I could read lips from all the way across the street.
She'd been astonished when I'd proved it to her.

"You have an amazing gift," my teacher had said.

I hadn't thought of it much since—it was just me. But
maybe it was a gift after all.

"So, can you read lips from that far away?" Patrice asked
again.

Demanding little prep, wasn't she? I nodded. "Yeah. Not
all the time, though. If a person doesn't speak clearly, it
looks like they are mashing their lips together. Or if they
have mustaches." I waved a hand at the teacher.

Patrice leaned back in her seat. "What did they say?"

"Mrs. Weber told him not to call her at home, and he
said something about needing her and that he loved her."

The other girls babbled among themselves, but Patrice
smiled and looked at me with calculating eyes. "That's pretty
cool," she said. "I wonder if I could blackmail Mr. Bernard

into letting me skip running laps or something." She laughed when she said it, but her eyes glinted.

Elation filled me like I'd won a prize or something, but I didn't know why. These were preps, for crying out loud. Like they'd be friends with a chick with black nail polish and a pierced eyebrow.

Rachel turned to me. "That's so cool! Can all deaf people do that?"

I shook my head. "Nah—I'm really good at it. And like I said, I don't get everything. It depends on how the person talks."

Patrice leaned over and whispered something into Sonar's ear. I couldn't see what she said, but Sonar's response was very clear.

"She is *so* not our kind of girl. Can't you hear how weird she talks?"

Patrice leaned back and I looked away, not wanting to see her response. Just like preps the world over. Effing mean.

Rachel stood and grabbed her tray. "That's awesome. What class do you have next?"

My cheeks still burned from Sonar's comment while I checked my schedule. "Biology with Higgens."

"I'm going that way. Come on, I'll show you where your class is."

I slung my backpack over my shoulder and picked up my tray. Okay. Maybe they weren't all heartless bitches. That would be a first. It was rather . . . cool. Maybe I'd actually found a friend and wouldn't have to disappear into the crowd.

Someone bumped against me just as I reached the tray drop-off. The tray I was holding with one hand tipped. I tried to compensate by jerking it the other way, but my hand slipped. The tray spun one way and the plate containing the barely touched chili dog flew the other. The plate slammed to the floor and bounced, sending soggy bun and beans everywhere. They splattered across the front of my hoodie, but even worse, the greasy mess flung onto the kid who'd bumped into me. Pieces of bun decorated the front of his plaid shirt and a lone bean stuck to his collar.

"Watch where you're going!"

My face flamed. Stricken, I peered up into the dark, intense eyes of the guy I'd smiled at in class. Oh. My. Gawd.

His eyes fixed on me and his anger faded. "Hey, I know you."

I looked wildly around the room. Rachel looked sympathetic, but the other girls were laughing. Sonar looked me up and down and smirked.

How come I can never think of a snappy comeback at times like this? Something funny and cool that would show everyone just how little I cared. Instead I stood there like a moron with my face turning redder by the second.

"Nice going," I muttered, and, whirling around, fled from the cafeteria. My heart pounded in my chest and I didn't stop running until I burst through the wide doors that exited out of the school. No way would I start crying like a baby in front of all those people.

Once I reached the sidewalk, I took several deep gulps of air, trying to calm my racing heart. So much for fitting in.

I trudged home, glad I lived within walking distance from the school. A point Mom had driven into the ground when trying to persuade me the move was a good thing.

Mom wouldn't be too mad that I'd skipped the rest of the day, and I didn't care if she was. I'd had enough. Anyway, all I had to do was whine and she'd be fine. Whining almost always won Mom over. Sometimes I even felt guilty about it. *Sometimes.* Usually I felt as though I deserved whatever I was whining about because I put up with the smothering. I mean, Mom had even asked me if I wanted her to come into the building with me this morning. As if! Like that wouldn't stick out—Mommy walking the little deaf girl into school. Gawd.

In fact, one of the only things Mom hadn't caved in to was not moving when I begged her to stay. Then she had decided to grow a spine of steel. So here I am, a walking advertisement for Dennison's chili.

Pissed off, I kicked a rock on the sidewalk. What I really wanted to do was fling it through a window or something.

I paused before going through the gate that led to my new home. At least the house had been an awesome surprise, though I wasn't about to tell my parents that I'd fallen in love with it the moment I'd seen it. It would give them *way* too much satisfaction. The house looked like something out of a Southern movie that had been transplanted out West. An emerald green lawn bordered the large white house. A brick walkway led to a spacious covered porch outfitted with a swing built for two. Perfect for making out. The dark-haired boy flashed through my mind.

Well, I'd blown that.

"Mom?" I called, swinging into the house. "You home?" I walked into the kitchen, carefully pulling my hoodie over my head. I shook out the few beans still sticking to it over the sink.

Someone tugged on my hair from behind and I turned to find Mom smiling at me. "I'm right here, pumpkin. How come you're home so early?" The toxic scent of paint thinner wafted up from the towel in her hand.

I held my nose. "Eww! I hate that stuff."

"I know. That's why I waited till you were gone to paint." She leaned forward and plucked at my hair. "Is that a bean?"

"Yeah. About that . . ."

"Okay, spill it. Though it looks as if you've spilled something already." Mom took my hoodie. "Actually, you better go change first. It looks like you have more gunk on your jeans, too."

I slipped out of my jeans and headed up to my room to change.

A few minutes later I came back down dressed in comfy shorts and one of my dad's old T-shirts. Mom sat curled up on the couch with cold drinks for both of us.

She patted the couch beside her. "So why don't you tell me why you came home early wearing your lunch?"

Oh gawd. The heart-to-heart. I hated them, and they seemed to come with increasing frequency lately. She was worried about me, she didn't approve of my choice of friends, she didn't like my clothes. There was always something. Whatever.

Though, on second thought, I could use some sympathy about now. Mom was always great for sympathy, so I filled her in. "I felt like an idiot. And the girls were sorta nice to me. At least, Rachel was," I said, remembering the nasty comment about the way I talk.

"I don't think it's going to be such a big deal. Everyone will probably forget about it by tomorrow."

"Would you have forgotten something stupid like that when you were in high school?" I demanded.

Mom hesitated.

"Aha!" I hit her with a couch cushion.

"It'll blow over, I promise." She pulled the couch cushion from my hand and held it close to her. "So tell me what the girls were like."

Mom, with her glossy brown hair, perfect skin, and perfect teeth, had spent her high school years as a cheerleading homecoming queen. Telling her the girls were popular would just get her hopes up. I knew she wished I were more like that, and I hated it. I wanted to scream at her, "I'm deaf and I talk funny! Cheerleaders don't hang out with girls like me!"

But Mom was always so hopeful. I hated disappointing her.

I rolled my eyes. "Just some girls, Mom. You know, dresses, hair, perfume . . ."

By the time I finished showering and changing, my dad had come upstairs from work. One of the reasons the 'rents had bought the house was its large daylight basement. Mom's first project was to redo the basement, turning it into an office for Dad and Uncle Alan's new consulting business. Which is why the scent of paint thinner clung to everything in the house.

Even though the smell made me want to vomit, I couldn't wait to get started on my room. I planned on using vivid colors with an anime theme.

I followed my parents out to the car. Mom and Dad had insisted on some kind of welcome dinner at Aunt Shirley and Uncle Alan's. They'd just come home from vacation, and everyone had decided it was time for family togetherness. Something else to look forward to. Not. Mom said I needed to get to know my cousins, but I was in the mood to feel sorry for myself and dinner with kidlets put a serious kink in my plans.

The car sped out of town and the road wound its way up out of the valley.

I leaned forward. "I thought they lived in town."

"They did," her dad replied. "They moved up here last year so Aunt Shirley could continue her work."

"What does she do?" I asked.

"She runs a no-kill shelter for dogs. She wanted to save cats as well, but Alan put his foot down." I could see Dad chuckling in the rearview mirror. "I didn't think my brother could tell her no about anything."

I giggled, in spite of my resolve to be sullen for the evening. Talking to my parents was such a relief after straining to hear other people all day. They always pitched their voices lower and spoke louder, so I caught almost everything they said.

The car turned onto a long dirt road. Several outbuildings came into view, including a shiny new barn. It dwarfed the ranch-style home next to it.

"I think when they took in Miller, Shirley felt like she could expand the shelter," Mom said. "I guess he's a huge help."

"Who's Miller?"

"The young man who's living with them."

Dad parked the car as three or four dogs came running out, barking wildly. I reached up and turned my hearing aids down. Two young, barefoot boys ran out the door. I could see them yelling at the dogs, but it didn't seem to make much difference.

When my aunt and uncle came out of the house, they swept me up into their arms like a long-lost relative. Which in a way, I guess I was. There was too much going on, though, and I missed almost everything they said until we were in the house.

Aunt Shirley led me and Mom into the kitchen. She turned back to me. "So how are the girls treating you? Everyone being nice?"

Her glance was sharp and carried far more meaning than the question deserved.

"Everyone is great. Why?"

"Just let me know if anyone bugs you and I'll take care of it. I still have school connections."

She looked deep into my eyes and I moved backward. Who was she, the freaking Godfather?

She laughed and turned back to her work. She directed the rest of the conversation to my mother, and though I'd turned my hearing aids up, I couldn't hear what she was saying. The chatter of the children underfoot, along with the clanging of pots and pans, made listening impossible. I backed out of the kitchen and went to find Dad and Uncle Alan. I caught a glimpse of them disappearing down a long hallway. Probably going to talk about work stuff. I sped up to catch them. It would be boring, but better than the kitchen chaos.

Oomph! I ran headlong into something both soft and solid. I stumbled backward, but before I could fall, a strong pair of arms steadied me.

My heart raced as I looked up into a pair of familiar brown eyes. They lit up as if a fire had been kindled behind them.

"We just keep running into each other, don't we?" he said.

Two

Why did I eat so much? My stomach protested against my jeans with every step I took. And why did *this* guy have to be *that* guy?

Dinner had been a nightmare. Every time I had looked up, Miller's gaze had slid away from me. He had wrapped himself up in an uncomfortable silence the minute everyone gathered in the dining room. Better to keep my head down and shovel in the food. Good thing I like Mexican. Or *did*. Right now the thought of ever eating another burrito made me wanna barf.

Then Aunt Shirley's fateful words: "Miller, why don't you take Serena out and show her the kennels?"

I pretended not to hear, but Mom repeated it. Loudly. Thanks tons, Mom. I owe ya.

Miller's down-turned mouth had showed he was as excited about the prospect as I was.

The sun dipped lower in the sky, casting long shadows across the yard. Inked-out trees dwarfed the barn beneath them. I stole a glance at him but the shadows blurred his expression. They couldn't hide how hot he was, though.

"Did you get full?" he asked, his voice clipped and polite.

I jumped. Had he caught me staring? And, omigod, he'd noticed me pigging out.

"Yeah, I was hungry. I didn't eat a lot of lunch," I said.

He burst out laughing. "I noticed."

I giggled even though I could feel my cheeks heating up. Looking back on it, it had been pretty funny.

I relaxed and followed him into the barn. Only a dim light glowed in the background and I squinted, trying to make out the dark shapes against the walls.

"I can't see. Is there another light?" I turned and ran right into Miller. Again. His hands steadied me, and for a moment neither of us moved. The same electricity I'd felt when he had looked at me in class coursed through my body.

He leaned toward me in the darkness, his face inches away from mine. "Hold on," he said, his mouth so close to my ear that his breath whispered across my neck. I shivered.

He reached up behind me and flicked a switch. The barn flooded with light and I blinked. His hand still warmed my shoulder and I wondered what it would feel like if he let his hand trail up my throat and cup my chin.

His eyes caught mine and I lowered my gaze, sure he'd be able to see right through me.

"Where are the dogs?" I asked, looking around the room. What was up with me? It wasn't as if I'd never been kissed. I was pretty experienced. Girls who hung out with guys all the time generally were, but I'd never felt my legs turn to liquid butter before. Never longed to run my hands over someone's arms or chest. I shook my head. Enough!

My nose twitched. The overwhelming scents of dogs and hay hung in the air, though I smelled an underlying scent of antiseptic as well. Cages lined one wall and stacks of shelving lined another.

"This room is for sick dogs and supplies. None of them are sick right now."

I turned toward him, loving the way he spoke. His perfectly pitched voice allowed me to hear much of what he said and his lips enunciated the words cleanly. *Don't think about his lips*, I told myself sternly.

I noticed an examining table in one corner standing next to a glass case filled with medical supplies. "You treat them here?"

"We treat a lot of stuff on our own, though we call the vet for anything too weird. I work part time for the vet, so he does most everything for free. Come on, I'll show you the big dogs."

I followed him through another door. The barking made me wince and I turned my aids off.

I saw him notice the action with raised eyebrows, but he didn't comment on it.

"Too loud," I explained, liking that he didn't ask me a million questions about being deaf. "It becomes a wall of sound in my ears and I really can't pick anything out."

He turned to face me. "I know how to shut them up." He walked over to a barrel and opened the lid. "Here, grab some."

I looked into the barrel before shoving my hand in.

"What? You don't trust me?" The innocence of his widened eyes contrasted with his crooked grin.

I scooped out a handful of dog biscuits. "Not really. Trust isn't part of my nature."

He grinned and slipped a dog biscuit through the fencing. A large multicolored boxer took it out of his hand gently and carried his prize over to a blanket on the floor to eat.

"We call this one Brutus." He pointed to the boxer. "Someone found him wandering around on the freeway and brought him to us."

My mouth dropped open as I watched the beautiful, sleek animal enjoying the last few crumbs of his treat. "You mean somebody dumped him?"

The dog rose up and meandered over to Miller, who rubbed under his chin. Miller's gentle manner showed how much he loved the animal. "Yeah, happens all the time. Sometimes we get a dog because their owners can't keep them for some reason, but usually they're abandoned."

I knelt and shoved a couple of bones at twin black Labs. Miller fed the rest of the dogs and they immediately quieted down. Some curled up on their blankets to sleep while others stuck their noses through the cages begging for attention. I flipped the volume of my hearing aids back up.

Miller knelt next to me and my heart pinged at his nearness. He smelled like pine trees, fresh hay, and something infinitely male. What would he do if I leaned into his neck for better sniffage? I grinned.

He led me into another room and we handed out smaller treats to the little dogs. Did he feel the tingle up his arm when he touched my hand? 'Cause everything he did made me tingle. I glanced at his face, but his dark eyes were as unreadable as midnight.

He showed me the puppy room, with its big bins filled with sawdust, and finally the cleaning room, packed with supplies to keep disease from spreading.

"This must cost a fortune," I said as we entered the main room again.

He faced me. "It does. Luckily, we haven't had to hire anyone full time and we get the vet care for free. Food and supplies are our biggest costs. Shirley inherited some money, so she was able to build the place, but keeping it running is a whole 'nother ball game."

My parents walked into the barn with Aunt Shirley and

Uncle Alan. Miller's face, which moments before had been lively and passionate, suddenly shuttered. "I have to go," he muttered, and walked out the door.

Miller was the last thing on my mind when I went to sleep and the first thing I thought of when I woke up. He was a puzzle. A puzzle I'd like to assemble piece by delicious piece. I stretched and allowed myself to laze in bed for a couple more precious minutes.

What had happened? At dinner he had sat all brooding and sullen but then did a quick turnaround when we were alone. After everyone rejoined us, he went all standoffish and pissy again. What was up with that?

I wrapped my arms around my pillow. My other guy friends, even the ones I had made out with on occasion, had never treated me the sweet way he had when we were alone. He had always faced me when he spoke and tapped my shoulder when he wanted to get my attention, but he hadn't talked about himself at all. So why did he turn all weird again the minute we were with other people?

And how had he come to live with Aunt Shirley and Uncle Alan in the first place?

I hopped out of bed and dressed in a hurry. My room looked like more of a storeroom than a bedroom. Boxes stood stacked almost to the ceiling against one wall, and my clothes had been flung over most of the floor. Mom had promised she'd start on the painting today.

I considered the collection of hoodies I'd thrown onto my bed. It still felt like summer outside, which made a hoodie a little warm. And no one else wore one . . . Oh, the hell with it. I grabbed a blue one and defiantly yanked it over my head. Like anyone would talk to me after yesterday anyway.

Except for Miller. Just thinking of him made my stomach flip.

I blew a kiss at my unfinished room. "Will get to you soon," I promised before heading downstairs.

"Mom? How come Miller is living with Aunt Shirley?" I asked once I reached the kitchen.

Mom rubbed her eyes and leaned against the kitchen counter. "Huh?"

Mom was so not a morning person. I waited until she'd taken a couple sips of coffee before asking again. "So why is Miller living with them?"

"Mmph." Mom opened one eye. "You want an Americano or juice?"

"Americano. Tell me."

Mom held up her hand while she brewed the espresso shot and poured in the boiling water. "You're going to stunt your growth." She handed me the steaming cup.

I poured some cream into it and stirred. "Mom, I'm small and curvy. I'll be small and curvy till the day I die." I raised my eyebrows and gave a meaningful look at Mom's tiny waist, full bust, and hips. "It's genetic, thank you very much. Now about Miller . . ."

Mom plopped down at the kitchen table and gave a giant yawn while saying something.

I gritted my teeth. "I can't hear you when you yawn. What did you say?"

"Oh, sorry. I asked how come you're so interested in Miller?"

Couldn't she just answer the bloody question? "My aunt and uncle practically adopt a teenager and I don't have a right to be curious?"

"Eh, I guess. They took him in after his mom died. He'd been helping with the dogs at their old house when his mom got sick. I guess she suffered with cancer for about a year before dying. She asked Shirley and Alan if they would take care of him until he was old enough to go off to college. Very sad."

My stomach dropped at the thought of being all alone in the world. "He didn't have any other family?"

"Apparently not." Mom laid her head on the table with a little sigh, which pretty much meant conversation over till Dad came down to make her breakfast.

I sipped my coffee. Gawd, what a bummer. I knew all too well what it was like to be alone in the world. No matter how well I read lips or how high powered my hearing aids were, I was always going to be different. One technical malfunction could silence my whole world. Now *that* was lonely.

I gathered my school stuff and set out. The clear autumn sky promised another warm day. Back home, leaves would be turning deep orange or red, and the mornings would be crisp. Here the leaves were a tired green, as if they'd be relieved to change colors and drop off. The wind picked up, blowing my hair in my face. Great—I'd probably arrive at school looking like a scarecrow, with my hair sticking out all over the place. I pulled my brush out of my backpack and tried to hold my hair with one hand. I stepped out into the street to cross.

Suddenly a horn blared. I fell back on my butt as a red Mustang swerved, missing me by mere inches.

"You ass!" I screamed at the car. I crawled to the sidewalk, dragging my backpack behind me. I huddled there, my head buried in my arms, all of Mom's overprotective warnings sounding in my head over and over.

"No street hockey—you can't hear the cars."

"No, you can't learn to ride a bike—it's too dangerous."

"You have to look both ways before you cross the street and keep looking. No one's going to watch out for you—you have to do it yourself."

Mom's warnings always felt like a smothering blanket she was trying to wrap me in, but maybe she'd been right all along.

I wiped my eyes. Great. I probably had makeup streaking down my face. Bloody freaking hell.

I stood, my legs still shaking, and headed for school.

The near miss with the car screwed up my entire morning.

The only good thing was that no one mentioned the chili

dog incident from the day before. Maybe Mom had been right about that, too. Maybe everyone really would forget.

I bounced into American history, feeling better. At least Miller would be here.

Rachel smiled when I sat in my seat and I smiled back. "Lunch again today?"

I hesitated. What if Miller asked me to have lunch with him? Then I shrugged and nodded. Why not? Miller probably sat with his own friends.

I darted a glance over to where he sat, but he wasn't there yet. I pulled out my history book and turned to the page Ms. Fisher had written on the board. At least Ms. Fisher hadn't tried to waylay me with more sign language. Ha! She'd barely acknowledged my existence. Just how I like it. Under the radar.

A jolt of electrical current ran through my body when Miller walked through the door. Gawd, couldn't he feel it?

I caught his eye and flashed a smile. He nodded impersonally and sat at his desk.

He didn't look at me again.

Hurt erupted in my stomach and flowed into my chest. What did I do? I recalled how closed he'd become when everyone walked into the barn. Had I pissed him off somehow?

I turned to my work. Whatevah. I had better things to do with my time than to worry about him. *Note to self: Guys are jerks.* I concentrated so hard on my work that I didn't even notice that everyone had left until Rachel tapped me on the shoulder.

"You wanna go to lunch or do you wanna stay here all day?" Rachel grinned, showing off perfect dimples in cover-girl skin.

Okay, I was big enough to admit that the pang in my chest was jealousy. I usually didn't get jealous of girls like her. We weren't even in the same league, but Rachel's pink and gold coloring made me feel dark and sullen. Like a toad next to a water lily. I wondered what it would be like to wake up to that face in the mirror every morning.

"I'm coming, I'm coming," I said, following her out into the hall.

Same table, same girls. I suddenly felt sort of shy, remembering the great chili-dog caper of the day before. A couple of the girls gave me friendly nods while the others looked amused.

"You're not wearing your chili today?" one girl asked, snickering.

I tilted my chin. I'd taken on worse than her. "No, I left it on my other hoodie. But thanks for asking, Sonar. It *is* Sonar, right?"

The shouts of laughter around the table clued me in that it probably wasn't Sonar. Names could be hard to understand. I'd spent too much time learning regular words to be concerned with people's names. I felt a hot blush moving its way up my neck and face. So much for showing off my clever comebacks. I looked up as Patrice sat down next to me.

"It's Sonya. Son-ya," Patrice said. "Don't worry about them—they can be be-yotches." She wrinkled her nose at her friends and they made faces back. They also stopped laughing.

Any question who led the welcoming committee?

"Wanna soda?"

Leave it to Rachel to change the subject.

"Sure." I dug around in my jeans but Rachel stopped me.

"Nah, I got this one."

I smiled at her. "Thanks."

Patrice nibbled on a piece of lettuce. "So are you liking the school?"

"Yeah, it's not too bad," I said. "Different from my old school."

"Did you go to a special school?" Sonya asked with a smirk.

My throat closed at Sonya's thoughtless question. Like being deaf made me stupid.

"Nah, just your average, ordinary high school, like this one. Except it was in the city and we got to do a lot of cultural things, like plays, museums, fashion shows, and stuff like that."

So there. I took a bite of salad. Sonya's down-turned lips showed the comment had hit its mark.

I smiled a thank-you at Rachel as she set my soda in front of me. Patrice turned away and started a conversation with Kelly on her other side. I looked around the table and noticed Sonya casting a sideways glance at Patrice. She leaned over to Kayla and I focused on their lips.

"Looks like someone's having a bad hair day."

Kayla leaned over. "Patrice?"

Sonya nodded. "Whoever told her she didn't need bangs obviously hadn't seen the widow's peak from hell."

I looked around the cafeteria. A red-haired girl detached herself from a crowd and walked over to our table. She stood next to Sonya and waited to be noticed.

I saw Sonya's eyes flick over to where the girl stood and then turn back to Kayla. What a bitch. Kayla's eyes kept sweeping over to where the girl stood, but she didn't say anything.

Finally Sonya turned and raised her eyebrows. "Yes?"

The girl gave a tentative smile. "I brought you something. You and Patrice."

Patrice looked up expectantly.

Sonya held out her hand and the girl handed her a card, then walked over and gave one to Patrice. "Starbucks cards," she said. "I thought maybe you guys would like them." She stretched her lips into a nervous smile.

Patrice smiled. "You can never have too many Starbucks cards."

Sonya shrugged. "I'll put it with my other ones. Doesn't your brother work there or something? I saw him scrubbing the toilets last time I was there."

The girl flushed. "Yeah, he does." She backed away from the table. "I hope you like them."

Sonya rolled her eyes at Patrice. "Yeah, like we'd ever let her in," she said when the girl was out of earshot.

Into what?

Patrice snorted and changed the subject. "So who's going to the football game tomorrow night?"

The girls all chorused affirmatively.

"You should come with," Rachel said, turning to me.

"You'd have a blast," Patrice confirmed.

Wow. I hadn't seen that one coming. Preps asking the deaf punk girl to a game with them.

Sonya jumped in. "She probably wouldn't like it."

What. A. Bitch.

A long silence ensued and the girls exchanged uncomfortable looks.

Rachel leaned forward to say something, but I interrupted. I'd been fighting my own battles way before Rachel came along.

"You mean the way you don't like Patrice's hair?" I asked, giving Sonya a big fake smile. "Didn't you mention a widow's peak from hell?"

Sonya turned a bright red as Patrice touched her hair.

Uh-huh. That's what I'm talking about.

I stood up. Who was I kidding? I'd never fit in. No use even trying. Patrice's hand on my arm stopped me.

"I'd love for you to come tomorrow night," she said firmly, standing up next to me. "I'll pick you up in my car."

Rachel gave my other arm an excited little squeeze.

"I'd love to," I said, looking at Sonya. "Can't wait."

I took off, carrying my tray. Gawd, was having girl-friends really worth the fuss? Guys were so much easier. Or were they? I stopped so quickly that Rachel, close behind, rammed me in the back with her tray.

"Oops, sorry," she said close to my ear.

I didn't answer. My heart gave a little leap. Miller stood next to the tray-dumping station clearing his lunch tray.

I boldly stepped up next to him. "Hi, Miller. How's it going?"

He turned with a small, remote smile that faded when he noticed Rachel behind me.

"Hey," he muttered, and sped off.

I watched him go with my mouth open. What happened to the electricity? The sweaty palms? The quick, meaningful glances? Was that even the same guy?

Rachel came up alongside me and dumped her tray. "Don't mind him. He's always been that way."

"Have you known him long?"

"All our lives. One of the things that come with living in a small town—you know too much about everyone." Rachel wrinkled her nose. "Miller's always been a bit of a loner. He's gotten worse since his mom died. Fights and getting in trouble with the teachers—stuff like that. Most of us just leave him alone."

Very interesting, I thought, remembering how easily he'd spoken to me in the barn last night.

I glanced back across the cafeteria. Patrice and Sonya were having a heated argument. I tuned in as soon as I saw my name mentioned.

Patrice's pretty face was animated. "Do you know how much dirt she could dig up for us? She should totally be in the sorority."

"You're kidding me, right?" Sonya turned her face away before I could find out exactly what she thought Patrice was kidding her about.

Rachel tugged on the sleeve of my hoodie. "Are you coming?"

I turned and followed Rachel, my mind racing. "What sorority were they talking about?"

Rachel blinked. "What? How did you know . . . oh, right, you read lips." Her eyes darted around the hallway like she was afraid of being overheard.

Gawd, what was up with all the secrecy? "If you don't want to tell me, no biggie."

"No, it's just that it's sort of a secret and I could totally get my butt chewed and initiation week is coming up—" Rachel clamped her hand over her mouth. "Look, I promise I'll tell you later, but not at school, okay?"

What was with this freakazoid school, anyway? I agreed, and with another anxious glance around us, Rachel scurried off to her next class.

Three

"You are not following me to the football game and I am *not* wearing too much eyeliner!"

I stomped back to where Mom sat at the computer.

"Calm down." She barely glanced up from the screen. "We're going because we want to be a part of the community, not because we want to spy on you."

"I don't believe you!" Not with Mom's track record, a record that included going to my first junior high dance, my first day of mainstreamed high school, and even all my field trips. Parent helper. Right. "So how come you didn't mention community togetherness until *after* I told you I'd been invited to the game?"

"I promise I won't even look your way. We'll be with Shirley and Alan. And you *are* wearing too much eyeliner."

Unreasonable. Totally unreasonable. I almost called Dad up out of his office to mediate, but that wouldn't have done any good. He left stuff like this up to Mom.

"Go get *Seventeen* or something and check it out. I'm not wearing any more eyeliner than anyone else." I knew I had a better chance of keeping the eyeliner than I did of keeping Mom away from the football game. Gotta pick your battles.

"Last time I checked, you were sixteen, not seventeen. If you had any more eyeliner on, you'd be a raccoon. And why do you wear such dark clothes? Why don't you try wearing something lighter?"

My teeth ached from gritting them so hard. "What's wrong with my clothes? My clothes are just fine!" I knew I sounded hysterical, but honestly!

Mom turned to face me completely. "There's nothing wrong with the way you dress. I just want you to fit in, honey."

I threw up my hands and flipped my hearing aids off. Conversation over. I whirled around so I couldn't see Mom's lips.

"I can't hear you!" I yelled, and stomped upstairs to my bedroom.

I glared at the drop cloths covering my furniture. The revolting gray primer on my walls mocked me. Mom had insisted the dark red I'd chosen would look better if they used primer first, but right now my room both stunk and looked like crap.

It matched my mood.

Why did Mom do this? That mind-bending, air-sucking mother hover. Helicopter parenting to the max. It hadn't been so bad when I was a kid trying to mainstream into the hearing world, but now it made me feel like she had no confidence in me. As if I couldn't do anything on my own.

I glanced at my watch. Patrice had said she and Rachel would pick me up at six. That gave me about twenty minutes to finish getting ready.

Even school had been an exercise in frustration. Miller still wasn't talking to me, and Rachel hadn't mentioned a single word about the sorority. Not that I expected her to at school. *Mental note: Get Rachel alone to find out what the heck the sorority is and why it's such a big secret.*

I checked my makeup in the mirror, the one thing not covered by a cloth. My spirits lifted. The eyeliner looked good. I looked good. I tucked my dark hair behind my ears and then pulled it forward again to hide my hearing aids. When I'd started high school last year, I'd tried to get away with only wearing one so I could clip my hair back on one side. But, of course, my grades nose-dived 'cause I couldn't hear squat, and then Mom found out and that put an end to that.

I checked my watch again. Fifteen minutes.

Should I? I opened my jewelry box and took out a miniature ring with a small diamond on one side. Mom had convinced me not to wear my eyebrow ring at school. But this wasn't school, was it? Grinning wickedly, I clipped it in. It looked good.

I sat on the floor and flipped through the stack of giant

prints Mom had ordered before the move. Having an interior designer for a mother had its advantages. The five lithographs had inspired the color scheme of my entire room. Anime in its purest sense, they would light up the room with energy and color. With dark red walls and pearl gray carpeting and furniture, I'd finally get a room that went with my style and personality. We were going to work on it over the weekend.

Ten minutes. My stomach tightened with nerves. Going out with a group of preppies was different from hanging out at the skate park with a bunch of punks. Tonight I'd be with a group of girls. Like a normal teen, instead of a punk skater chick. Yeah, right. A normal teen with her mom shadowing her every move.

I sighed. Might as well go make up with the mother figure. I flicked my hearing aids back on and headed downstairs.

"Is Miller coming?" I asked. Mom and Dad were getting ready to go and slipping into light jackets.

"Oh, can you hear me now?" Mom raised her eyebrows.

I sniffed. "Yeah, though if you call me at the game, I'll pretend not to." I stuck my tongue out. Okay, sticking your tongue out at your parents was juvenile, but so satisfying.

Mom ignored it and my eyebrow ring, though I saw her eyes had flicked to it right away. "I think Miller's going. Why?"

So I can find out why he ignores me in school. "Oh, no reason, just wondering." I spied a white Jetta pulling up to the house. "Gotta go!" I grabbed my cell phone and made a dash for the door, but Mom grabbed the hood of my sweatshirt and stopped me short. Damn, I had almost made it.

"Not so fast. I'm going out to meet them." She flashed me a crooked grin.

Somebody stop this. Please. "Dad!" I pleaded.

He shrugged. "Sorry, it's our job to make you nuts."

"You don't look sorry," I shot over my shoulder before following Mom out the door.

Patrice and Rachel smiled at us as we came out to the driveway. Their parent faces were carefully assembled— open, respectful, and polite. They climbed out of the car as Mom introduced herself.

I checked out my parents with a critical eye as they chatted with my friends. I guess they weren't so bad . . . for parents. Whereas Dad was dark and rather plain looking, my vivacious mother wouldn't have looked out of place going to the game with us. Ewww.

"Oh, hey, we got something for you," Patrice said, reaching into the backseat of the car.

She took out a maroon and gold school hoodie with HILLSDALE HIGH BULLDOGS emblazoned across the front of it. Both Patrice and Rachel were wearing one.

"I love it!" I squealed. Oh gawd. Did I just squeal? I never squeal. Maybe preppiness was catching. I looked over at the perfection that was the other girls. Nah, I could never be like them, could I? I shook my head and peeled off my own hoodie, careful not to catch it on my eyebrow ring. I tossed it at Mom, who caught it deftly. I pulled the new sweatshirt over my head and fixed my hair.

"Now you look like one of us," Rachel said.

"It's fantastic," Mom said.

I glanced at my mom, suddenly suspicious. Were those tears in her eyes? "Is it time to leave?" I hurriedly opened the back door of the car and hopped in.

"We should be home by eleven," Patrice said, getting in and starting the car. "Sometimes a bunch of us stop at Jerry's Restaurant on the way home for something to eat. Is that okay?" Patrice flipped back her hair and dimpled up at my parents.

They gave their enthusiastic permission.

Man, she was good. Talk about a con artist.

Patrice pulled away from the house slowly with the radio on low. Two blocks away she hit the gas and cranked up the tunes. Rachel yelled something back to me, but I just pointed at my ears and shrugged. Not even hearing people would be able to hear over that noise.

I sat back and concentrated on the way the wind blew my hair around my face and how No Doubt sounded blasting in my ears. Okay, they sounded like a wall of noise, but the bass beat in my chest and for a rare moment I felt as though I belonged. I could get used to this.

All around us, students in other cars headed for the game, arms hanging out of open windows, hands tapping out tunes. Sometimes at stoplights kids hopped from car to car. My old high school hadn't been like this. Of course, I'd only gone to one football game, so maybe it had been and I'd just missed it. I'd missed a lot of things.

The car door suddenly swung open and Kayla and Kelly hopped in, giggling. Lots of talking—yelling, actually—over the stereo ensued. I didn't even try to figure it out.

Kayla and Kelly's mother obviously couldn't think of any names but those starting with *K*. Today at lunch I'd met their younger sisters, Katie and Kelsey. All four of them looked like Barbie's little sister. Not that I'd ever played with Barbies.

Rachel turned the stereo down and twisted around to face me. "You're gonna have fun. We don't watch a lot of the game, but it's fun anyway."

Kayla said something and laughed.

I couldn't hear her. "What?"

Kayla turned to me. "I said, we mostly just check out guys."

"Especially Patrice," Rachel said, grinning.

Patrice shook her finger as she pulled into the school parking lot. "Not just any guy—*the guy*."

"Who?" I asked, turning my aids up. Like I'd know who they were talking about.

"Scott!" Kayla and Kelly yelled as they crawled out of the car. Definitely loud enough to hear.

Teenagers milled about the parking lot while parents

with blankets and little kids strolled toward the field. A snack bar sold goodies and Bulldog keepsakes. We stopped for drinks on our way in.

"We'll get snacks later," Rachel explained. "But we'll be walking around until the game starts."

Cheerleaders kicked and strutted, trying to whip the players and the crowd into a frenzy of school spirit. People mostly ignored them, except for a rapt audience of drooling middle school boys.

I checked out my companions. They all looked as though they'd been born with pom-poms in their hands. "So how come you guys aren't cheerleaders?"

"We were," Patrice said. "We're boycotting."

"How come?"

"'Cause the PTA made us add an inch to the skirts." Patrice nodded her head at the cheerleading squad. "You notice that they found a bunch of dweebs to take our place. Losers who are more than willing to wear the longer skirt. We'll be back on the squad next year and make it rock again."

"But what about her?" I jerked my thumb toward Sonya, who paraded up and down in front of the other cheerleaders, shaking her pom-poms.

Rachel rolled her eyes. "Her mom's the president of the PTA. She didn't have a choice."

Patrice watched Sonya with a frown. "I think she's enjoying being squad leader. Never would have happened if I'd been on the team."

Kelly tapped Patrice's shoulder. "There he is." She pointed to a couple of football players talking on the sidelines. They held their helmets in their hands, and most girls probably thought they looked dangerously gorgeous.

They looked like blockheads to me.

Miller was more my type. Intense, smoldering eyes, slightly curly black hair, and sensitive features. Yum.

Patrice grabbed my arm. "I'm going to go wish him luck. Watch and see what he says when I walk away."

"What? I can't do that."

Patrice's eyes focused on her prize. "Come on, Serena, I gave you a hoodie and everything. You're not ungrateful, are you?"

Her meaning came through loud and clear. My throat went dry and I licked my lips. At least now I knew why she'd invited me to the game. "I'll try," I said.

Patrice beamed. "That's all I want. Thanks!"

She sashayed up to the guys, and I marveled that anyone as beautiful as Patrice would be worried about what a guy thought of her.

Patrice smiled as she talked to the football players, her slanty green eyes accented by the new bangs she'd come to school with that morning. When she finished, she glided away in such a manner that they couldn't help but watch.

I focused on their mouths. I didn't know which one was which but figured Patrice could figure that out.

"Nice ass," number 28 said.

"Nice everything," number 34 commented. "You gonna ask her to homecoming?"

Number 28 laughed. "I might. Depends on my mood—if I want to be elected to the homecoming court or . . . get laid."

Number 34 laughed and clapped his hand on number 28's shoulder. "Yeah. Patrice is perfect, but Sonya's a sure bet."

They turned away and jogged down to one of the goalposts where the players were congregating. I swallowed and my stomach rolled. That felt . . . icky. It wasn't that I'd never eavesdropped on conversations before. I had. I used to watch people talk at the little coffee shop around the corner from my old house. But that had been practice, right? I'd never shared what I had learned.

"Did you get anything?" Rachel asked, giggling.

Before I could answer Patrice practically skipped up to us, her pretty face vivid with excitement. "Well?"

I nodded. "Which one was Scott?"

"Number 28. Number 34 is his best friend, Craig," Patrice said.

Kelly and Kayla leaned in, their blue eyes wide in anticipation.

My stomach stopped rolling. I didn't have to tell everything I'd learned, did I?

I smiled at Patrice. "For one thing, he thinks you have a nice ass."

Patrice preened. "He's right—I do."

Rachel laughed and hit her shoulder. "Go on. What else?"

"He's thinking about asking you to the homecoming dance."

Patrice leaned back, and her nose wrinkled as she gave a satisfied grin. "I knew it! Who's good, girls?"

Kayla nodded. "You sure called that one."

Patrice turned her green eyes back to me. "Anything else?"

My eyes swiveled over to where Sonya strutted in front of the crowd, pom-poms held high. "Nothing really, just some stuff about the game," I said, sure the lie was written all over my face.

I bowed my head and sipped my drink, not even trying to keep up with the girls' excited babble.

A couple of older girls walked past. Sleek and sexy, of course. What was it with this place? Was everyone gorgeous?

"Hey, Patrice," one of them called. "Slumming with the sophomores?"

Patrice laughed. "You know what I'm here for."

The other girl grinned. "Gonna have your list to me in a couple weeks?"

Patrice nodded. "Not a problem."

"It better be a good one. You know what's at stake."

They wandered off and Patrice took a casual drink of her soda as Kayla, Kelly, and Rachel cast each other worried glances.

They were just full of secrets, weren't they?

The game started and it became too noisy to hear much of anything. I tried to watch, though, since the others talked and joked, waved at friends in the stands, and didn't pay much attention to me.

I saw Mom and Dad walking away from the snack bar holding chili dogs. Mom pretended not to see me and I rewarded her with a smile and a wave. Nice to have a connection. I didn't see Miller at all.

Bored, I started watching people around me. Most were focused on the game, but others, like Patrice and her friends, were more interested in gossiping and being seen. I caught snatches of conversations.

"God, if my parents knew, they would kill me. . . ."

"There's a party after the game. I snuck a bottle of rum from my parents' stash. . . ."

"Okay, don't tell anyone, but Karen told me . . ."

Maybe the kids in this town weren't so perfect after all. A swift rush of power flowed through me as I realized how much was going on that I had missed. Why hadn't I ever done this before? I could sink ships with this kind of information.

"Wanna go get something to snack on?" Rachel asked in my ear, making me jump. She laughed. "Didn't mean to scare you."

"Sorry, I got caught up in the game," I told her.

I followed the other girls and dumped my watery drink into an overflowing garbage can. They stopped for a moment to talk to Sonya. I ignored her. There was just something about her that creeped me out. Maybe it was her cold, reptilian eyes. She ignored me back.

The second half of the game passed in a blur. The other girls actually buckled down and got into it when the score got close. I yelled and cheered with the rest of them, though school spirit had never been my strong suit. It was kinda hard to cheer on a school where 99.9 percent of the student body ignored you. But here it was different. It was almost like I was a part of it.

The after-party at Jerry's was the same way. Like the rest of the girls, I made spitballs and blew them at the good-natured waitress's butt. I tried Rachel's salad and shared my fries. Winning the game had put everyone in a good mood.

"Serena, I have to tell you that your eyebrow ring is wicked cool," Patrice said, grinning.

It was the first time anyone had mentioned it. I'd started to think maybe I had made a mistake in wearing it. "Thanks. I got it last year."

Rachel leaned in close to inspect. "Did it hurt?"

"No worse than getting my ears pierced."

"Did your parents go ballistic?" Kelly wanted to know, her face alight with interest. I'd already started thinking of her as the nice twin.

I laughed, remembering the arguments. "Not too bad. A lot of kids in my old school had piercings. Doesn't anyone here have any?"

They shook their heads, and once again I had the creepy feeling of being transported to a different world. "Bizarre," I said.

"I'd love to get my belly button pierced," Rachel admitted.

"Ow!" Patrice said. Suddenly she rose up out of her seat and looked out the window. "Hey now. Who do we have here?"

I followed the direction of her gaze. The two football players from earlier were climbing out of a red Mustang.

The same red Mustang that had almost turned me into road pizza yesterday.

My chest tightened. I turned and stared at the Thousand Island dressing I'd been dipping my fries into. It suddenly looked disgusting and my appetite vanished.

Would they recognize me? The idiot girl crawling in the road? I was angry at myself for being embarrassed. It's not like it was my fault! My face flamed anyway.

Rachel leaned over to me. "Are you okay?"

I nodded, then shook my head. "Excuse me." I scooted out of the booth.

Please don't throw up. Please don't throw up. I hurried to the bathroom. Once there, I wet a paper towel under cold water and held it to my face.

Rachel followed me into the bathroom. "You don't look okay," she observed, handing me another paper towel.

"I feel like crap," I admitted. "I think I'm going to text my parents and get a ride home."

"Might be a good idea. You won't get any cell service in here, though; you'll need to go up front."

We walked out the door and I was practically bowled over by a small boy.

"Serena!" the boy yelled, looking up into my face.

I recognized my cousin. The little one. What was his name? Oh, Zach.

Rachel laughed. "You know this creature?"

"Rachel, this is my cousin Zach. Are your parents here?"

Zach shook his head. "Nope, I came with Miller."

Just my luck. Aunt Shirley or Uncle Alan could have given me a ride home, but I really wasn't up to asking Miller. I looked across the room to where Patrice and the others now sat with Scott and his blockhead friend. I made up my mind. Better to face Miller's silence than face that. Silence I could handle.

Miller came around the corner carrying a bag. "Zach, where did you . . ."

I wasn't gonna beat around the bush. "Have you guys eaten already?"

"Nah, we ordered to go before we left the game. Zach and I are just picking up."

Zach nodded his head up and down. Then he kept doing it. Up and down. Up and down. It made me dizzy.

"Can you drop me off at home, then? I'm not feeling good."

Rachel watched the head bobbing. "Is he okay?"

Miller glanced down. "Knock it off, Zach." He looked back up at me. "Sure, no problem. I have the truck right outside."

I turned to Rachel. "Tell the other girls I wasn't feeling well, okay?"

"Sure." Rachel waved at Zach. "See you later, Mr. Bobblehead."

I darted out of the restaurant, ignoring the odd look Miller gave me. If we'd been on speaking terms, I might have told him, but as it was . . . forget it.

I buckled Zach up. He'd continued nodding and now his face looked like melting plastic.

"Uh, is he gonna hurt himself?" I asked.

"Nah, his neck's made of rubber."

Silence filled the cab of the truck except for the low buzzing sounds Zach made as he bobbled.

Finally Miller shot me a sideways glance. "So are you liking it here?"

"It's not too bad," I replied, relaxing a little. "The teachers are pretty much the same as in my old school, but the girls are nicer. Though I have to ask, are there any skate punks in the school? Or has the administration banished them all?"

His laughter made my stomach flip. *Settle down*, I told it silently. *This guy has ignored me for two days.*

"I guess I'm the closest thing to a punk you'll find here."

I digested that for a moment, and then he said, "I see you've found some friends."

I wasn't sure what to make of that comment, but I did like talking to someone who spoke loudly enough to hear without reading lips. "Yeah, they seem pretty nice."

I noticed that Zach had fallen asleep in midbob against his car seat.

"Rachel is nice. Kelly and Kayla are stupid, Patrice is an insecure control freak, and watch out for Sonya—she's mean."

Why did he have to dis my friends? So he was right on target. So what? It's not like he'd gone out of his way to make me feel comfortable. "Huh. I don't see you with any friends."

Another silence.

"I don't go around acting like other people," he bit out. "That pretty much makes me a nonperson in a school dedicated to conformity. I didn't take you for the conforming type, either."

His words hung in the air a if maybe he now thought he was wrong about me. It stung and I crossed my arms over my chest. "Don't you think there's a difference between conforming and fitting in?"

Miller didn't answer as he turned onto my block and pulled to a stop in front of my house.

I hopped out of the truck, miffed.

"Nice hoodie," he called.

I slammed the door. So I had worn the same hoodie as everyone else was. That didn't mean anything! Jerk! I stomped up to my front door. And to think I wanted to be friends with him!

I paused to watch the rear lights disappear down my street.

So why did I feel so bummed?

Four

I woke up the next morning with a megapainful crick in my neck. Mom had decided the paint fumes would poison me if I slept in my room, so I'd curled up on the couch instead. I'd probably pay for it all day.

The sun burned brightly outside and I checked the time. Eight o'clock. That was the problem with school. It got you used to getting up early. Even on Saturdays.

Funny how Mom and Dad never lost the habit of sleeping in on the weekends, which was nice for me. It kept parental interruptions at a minimum in the morning. Almost as good as sleeping in. I yawned and slipped in my hearing aids. Usually I waited until after my shower to put them in. But considering the work we'd be putting in my room today, I might as well wait to shower. I'd be all stinky and painty later, anyway.

I pattered into the kitchen and brewed myself a quick

Americano. Sweats and my dad's T-shirts were my week-end wear of choice, and I quickly changed in the laundry room before heading out to sip my coffee. The French doors off the kitchen led onto a large deck overlooking a river. I leaned over the railing with my cup, enjoying the view.

Back home our yard had been tiny and the neighbors had been within spitting distance. Here the wide expanse of lawn swept downhill to the river. The hills on the other side of the river were dotted with trees instead of houses. I'd never had such a private backyard.

I closed my eyes and imagined me and my new friends lying out on lawn chairs. Barbecuing. Sipping cold exotic drinks. Nibbling on little tropical snacks. I hadn't had a party of my own since I'd been mainstreamed. It might be kind of nice. No one could throw a party like Mom.

I giggled at my own imagination and opened my eyes.

"Serena? Get in here—you have company." Mom's voice sounded sleepy and cross. Whoever it was had probably woken her up. Not good. No one messed with sleep-in Saturday.

I hurried into the kitchen and stopped short when I saw Miller.

What was he doing here? My face flushed and I tried not to think about my holey sweats and my unwashed hair pulled back haphazardly.

Mom waved her hand and yawned. "Get him breakfast or coffee or whatever. I'm going back to bed."

She shuffled out of the room, turned as if she was going to say something, then went on her way.

Miller's eyes widened and his eyebrows reached to his hairline. "Was that the same woman we had dinner with the other night?"

"She has a thing about mornings."

Miller shuffled his feet. I tapped my fingers lightly on the kitchen counter and waited for him to tell me what he wanted. After his parting shot the night before, I didn't feel obligated to make it easy on him.

"I bring peace offerings," he said finally, holding out a basket. "I shouldn't have said anything about your friends."

His lean face was set and unhappy, and he didn't look me in the eye.

I melted. "You didn't have to do that. It wasn't that big of a deal."

He shrugged. "It was rude, and it gave me a good excuse to come over."

I ducked my head and took the basket to hide the blush that I knew was coming. "What's in here?" I moved the towel to reveal a dozen or so homemade blueberry muffins. The warm, sweet aroma came off in waves and I sniffed deeply. "Mmm. Would you like some coffee?"

He nodded and smiled, causing his eyes to glow with warmth.

I smiled back, trying to ignore the fluttering in my stomach. He sat at the kitchen table and waited while I brewed some Americanos. Sitting across from him, I took a bite of a still-warm, fragrant muffin.

"These are amazing." I pushed the basket across the table. "Do you want some?"

He laughed. "Nah, I already had six or so, hot out of the oven. Shirley made them bright and early this morning."

"Brighter and earlier than this?" I asked.

"Yeah, some of us have things to do in the morning."

"Oh, right. The dogs."

He smiled. "Yeah, the dogs . . . dummy."

I went cold all over. "Don't call me dumb."

"I didn't mean . . ." He caught sight of my face. "Oh, God, Serena, I didn't think."

I took a deep, shuddering breath. "No, that's okay. I over-reacted. I'm sorry. It took me longer than other kids to learn to talk. The girls at the playground teased me for being 'deaf and dumb.'" I looked away so I wouldn't see the pity in his eyes. I reached back and rubbed my neck.

"Neck hurt?" he asked, draining his coffee.

"Yeah. I slept on the couch last night 'cause we're working on my room."

"Here." He stood and moved in behind my chair. I tensed when he put his hands on my neck. "Relax."

Right. That's easy for you to say—you don't have mega-volts of electrical energy running through your body.

His fingers gently worked the muscles in my neck and shoulders, sending blissful shivers down my spine. "I used to do this for my mom after she finished a long day at work."

"Mm-hmm," I managed, incapable of saying anything coherent. My heart, which had raced at his first touch, had slowed and I closed my eyes, giving in to the sensation.

He kneaded his thumbs into a knot and I moaned. I couldn't help it. It felt lovely, wonderful, stupendous. My mind boggled at the adjectives.

His fingers stopped kneading and I was about to say something when the tips of his fingers traced my jawline and throat with the touch of a feather. I stopped breathing as he moved the hair falling from my ponytail with whisper-light softness. I sensed rather than felt him move down toward my neck. *If he kisses the back of my neck I will melt, I will die, I will just* . . .

Suddenly Miller leaped away from me with the speed of lightning.

Disoriented, I opened my eyes.

"Good morning," my dad said dryly.

I jumped. Okay, a bit late, but considering I was very nearly a puddle of goo, I thought I did pretty well.

Miller grinned. "Neck feel better?"

"Yeah, thanks." I looked up at my dad. "I had a crick— the couch, you know."

"Oh, I *know*." Dad grabbed a bottle of water from the fridge and pattered back upstairs.

To cover my embarrassment, I pointed at a flat package on the counter. "What's that?"

Miller shrugged and fidgeted. "Another peace offering. The muffins were actually from Shirley, so they didn't count." He got up and handed it to me. "It's not that great—I did it in a hurry."

I unwrapped the package, taking care not to rip the paper.

I turned it over in my hands and gasped. It was a framed portrait of me, bent over and feeding one of the dogs a treat. The charcoal sketch caught me perfectly, my eyes gentle, a slight smile on my face, my hair falling forward. I looked . . . beautiful.

I blinked back tears. "It's . . . it's amazing."

"It's nothing," he said, red faced. "I was going to give it to you later, but Shirley told me you were working on your room this weekend, and after last night . . ." He paused. "I thought I would finish it up and bring it over."

I stared at the sketch. What had he been thinking when he'd drawn it? No matter how sarcastic his comments had been last night, he'd been thinking of me. "You're not going to believe how perfect it is," I told him, hugging the sketch to my chest. "Want to see my room?"

"Sure."

We headed upstairs, remembering to tiptoe past my parents' room. I cursed my scruffy appearance. I almost pulled the ponytail holder out of my hair, but decided not to. It would probably look worse.

Even the mirror was covered today, but I showed him

the paint we were using and a sample of the carpeting.

"Oh, and check this out." I opened my closet door and pulled out the prints I'd stashed for safekeeping.

He knelt on the floor and flipped through them one at a time. "These are fantastic. Where did you get them?"

"My mom ordered them from a little shop in Portland." I held up his sketch. "See, it's perfect."

"I should've done it in anime, though I couldn't compete with these."

"You do anime? I love that style."

He grinned at me. "I knew you weren't a prep."

I frowned. "No, I'm not, but don't dis who I choose to hang out with, okay?"

He got up from where he was kneeling. "Deal." He looked around and noticed my skateboard in the closet. "You skate?"

I nodded.

"That would explain you asking if there were any skate punks in school."

I laughed. "I haven't had much of a chance to skate here, though."

"Yeah, the skateboard craze sorta missed us. Hey, you want some help with your room today? I'm not doing anything until I have to exercise the dogs. And that's not till later."

He smiled. My heart pounded. Electricity and heart palpitations. What was it about this guy? "That would be awesome. We have a lot of painting to do and the trim still needs to be sanded down and primed."

"Great." He beamed at me, which did nothing to calm my racing heart.

I hid the prints back in the closet and got out the supplies.

"Why don't we sand the trim and then we can vacuum before we get the paint out?" Miller picked up some sandpaper, felt the grit, then selected another piece.

"You look like you know what you're doing." I took the sandpaper he handed me and started working on the trim around the closet.

Miller dragged a step stool up to the bedroom door and began sanding. He said something else, but with his head so close to the ceiling I couldn't catch it.

"What?"

He turned to me and spoke louder. "Oh, sorry. I said I have a lot of experience. We didn't have the money to have someone remodel our house, so we did most everything ourselves."

His steady brown eyes focused on the job, but his lips were flat.

He's remembering his mom. "Was it fun?" I asked, trying to keep it light.

He smiled, as if remembering. "Yeah, it was. Mom was extremely artistic but a total klutz when it came to house stuff, so I did a lot of it. She was always willing, though. One time she dumped an entire can of paint on the hardwood floor. We ended up just painting the floor." He laughed. "Turned out pretty nice, actually."

I grinned. "Sounds like something I'd do. What happened to the house?"

His face shuttered and I wanted to bite my tongue off.

"We sold it when she died. I wanted to offer some of the money to Shirley and Alan for taking me in, but they wouldn't have any of it. It's in the bank for when I go to college."

Sadness. I couldn't imagine getting along without Mom. The mother hover was way better than being motherless.

I was about to say something when Miller leaped off the stool.

Mom's head popped in through the doorway.

"Miller, how nice to see you. I didn't know you'd stopped by. Did Serena get you breakfast? Want some coffee?"

"No, I'm good, thanks."

"Let me know if you need anything." Her head disappeared from the doorway and we busted up laughing.

"Is she serious?" he asked.

"Yep. She has absolutely no recollection of talking to you at all."

"That's amazing."

Still giggling, we went back to sanding and worked in a warm silence until Mom joined us half an hour later. I couldn't believe how much work we were able to get done with Miller's help. I kept looking at him, liking the way his dark hair curled over his ears. At one point I looked up to find him watching me, his eyes a smoky black. The moment stretched out between us and my mouth went dry.

"What?" I asked finally.

"You have primer on your nose."

I rubbed my nose, still mesmerized by his eyes. "Do I?"

Mom laughed. "Okay, time for a break. Serena, why don't you go wash up while Miller and I make some lunch?"

I hurried to the bathroom and cleaned the primer off my face. I stared at myself in the mirror. Whom did he see when he looked at me? The girl in the sketch or the messy, unkempt girl in the mirror? I pulled the ponytail holder out of my hair and put on some mascara. The lip gloss I added looked too fussy and I wiped it off. "No reason to be obvious," I told my reflection before skipping downstairs.

"Better hurry—I think Miller's hungry. He's already eaten two toasted cheese sandwiches," Mom said.

"I was just happy she wasn't making chili." Miller winked at me as I sat down.

I rolled my eyes. "Very funny."

"Did I miss something?" Mom set a plate in front of me. "Oh, I think you have a text, hon. Your phone beeped while you were upstairs."

I grabbed my phone off the table and pushed okay.

Whatcha doing?

It was from Rachel. I smiled and texted in: *Painting my bedroom.*

I set the phone down and took a big bite out of my sandwich. Miller leaned back in his chair, obviously stuffed.

"Can I get your number?" I asked.

Silence. "I, uh, don't have a cell phone."

My jaw dropped. "You what?"

He glared at his empty plate and Mom shot me a dirty look. Well, come on, who didn't have their own cell phone? *Oh.* A kid whose mom died and who was living with other people. Duh.

My face grew hot and my throat closed. We just couldn't seem to get along for very long, could we? My phone beeped and I picked it up.

We're coming 2 help! Already on our way.

Oh gawd. I glanced at Miller's unhappy face and then at the front door. What would the girls say when they found the school loner sitting in my kitchen? Would they still like me? Want to hang out with me? I really wanted them to come over, but I liked spending time with Miller, too. My stomach dropped and I swallowed. The cheese sandwich suddenly lost its flavor. What was I gonna do?

I shifted in my seat. "Look, I'm really sorry."

He stood up and shrugged. "Don't worry about it. Are you ready to get started again?"

His words said not to worry about it, but the tightness of his mouth said something else. I looked down at my phone. "Um, yeah, but are you sure you want to? I mean, don't you have to go exercise the dogs or something?"

He raised an eyebrow. "Nah, I don't have to do that until later."

"Well, you've already helped so much."

The doorbell rang. "I'll get it!" I jumped up and sent my chair crashing to the floor. Not bothering to pick it up, I jetted into the front hall. I opened the door and Patrice and Rachel poured in, laughing.

"We're all done shopping and thought we might as well come over and help," Rachel said.

Patrice raised an eyebrow. "Rachel wants to help; I just wanted to show you my goodies."

Both girls stopped short and stared across the hall.

Miller was leaning up against the kitchen doorjamb, comprehension in his eyes.

"Don't mind me." He jingled his keys. "I have to go exercise the dogs or something."

I flinched at his words. Point taken.

He edged past the girls, not looking at me.

"Thanks, Miller," I called as he went out. Now I'd gone and hurt him twice, after he'd been so nice and drawn the sketch and brought me muffins and everything. My heart sank.

"How freakishly odd," Patrice said before he slammed the door. "What was he doing here?"

I chewed on my lip, and I could feel my cheeks growing hot. "Helping me with my room."

"Oh, well, never mind that. Look at my stuff." Patrice

dumped her bag out on the hall table and I pretended to be awed by pastel Ts and short-waisted jackets.

"Why don't we go check out your room?" Rachel suggested.

Patrice repacked her bag and then we headed upstairs, but not before Patrice stuck her head through the kitchen door to say hello to my mom. You had to hand it to Patrice. She never missed a trick.

We got to my room and Patrice turned in a circle, looking at the mess.

"Okay, I see dark gray, a hideous reddish pink color, and white. Oh, honey, you need an interior decorator but bad."

My mom came in the door and laughed.

I snickered. "Um, my mom *is* an interior decorator."

Patrice's face fell and her mouth made a little O of surprise.

Rachel squeaked like a teapot, then, not able to hold them back, let out uncontrollable giggles.

Mom grinned. "Don't worry about it. It does look like a mess. My job is to make it all come together in the end. This is just the process."

She showed the girls the paint chips, swatches, and samples of what would soon be my room.

"When you're working with a red as deep as this, you have to paint on three or four coats before it becomes the true color you want," Mom said.

I tried to judge if Patrice's interest was real or not. I could never tell. "When I first opened the can of paint, I freaked," I said. "I thought my room would end up the color of Barney the dinosaur."

Rachel laughed.

"Could you do my room?" Patrice asked suddenly.

So the interest wasn't faked.

Mom looked pleased. "I have to finish my house first, and you'd have to ask your parents, but I was thinking of doing some freelance decorating after I'd gotten settled."

Patrice nodded. "My parents will love it. They'll do anything to get me to clean my room."

"So where do we start?" Rachel rubbed her hands together.

I pointed at the two of them. "In those clothes?"

Patrice looked down at herself. "These *are* Seven jeans. I'll pass."

"Do you have any old clothes we can use?" Rachel asked.

"Sure, if you want. I have some old sweats and another painting shirt."

Patrice held up a hand. "Not me. I'm into watching." She sat down on the step stool carefully and grinned at us.

"I'm game," Rachel said.

After Rachel changed, Mom showed us what to do and left us to it.

Patrice said something, but her voice was too soft. I turned, my face reddening. "Patrice, I'm sorry, but I can't understand what you're saying. I'm not facing you, so you're going to have to talk louder."

"I was just saying how awesome it was what you did for me last night. Finding out what Scott said and everything." She studied her fingernails. "I was wondering if you could do that again."

I stopped painting. "What do you mean?"

Patrice shifted on her seat. "Oh, nothing, really. I just want to find out what they are saying about me. That lip-reading stuff is cool, like mind reading or something. I think it would come in handy if you could do stuff like that for me sometimes." She twitched her shoulders.

I wrinkled my forehead. I *so* knew what she was driving at. "Read lips for you? Like in that one episode of *Seinfeld*?"

"I love that show!" Rachel exclaimed. "Did you see the one—"

"Exactly," Patrice interrupted and Rachel fell silent. "We can call it Operation Read My Lips or something."

I thought about it for a moment. Lip-reading for someone else's fun?

Patrice gave me a long, considering look before tossing her hair back and smiling. "Oh, and I forgot to tell you, we're throwing a homecoming party at my house next week. I'd love for you to come."

A party? I'd been invited to a party! But would Patrice still want me to come if I said no? I chewed my lip, stalling for time. But why say no? It wasn't so bad—a bit of lip-reading in exchange for a party. Rachel widened her eyes and nodded her head behind Patrice. "That would be awesome," I said finally. "I'd love to go."

Patrice beamed. "I knew you would!" Her cell phone rang and she answered it. Her eyes shot over to me. "I'm actually at her place right now. Hold on." She stood and moved toward the door. "I'm just going to take this out in the hall."

As soon as she left, Rachel jumped up and grabbed my arm. "Oh my God! I think she's going to ask you to join! It has to be that, or else she wouldn't have asked you to her party."

Okay, I was seriously confused. "Join what exactly?"

Rachel dropped my arm when Patrice came back in.

"Hate to do this, Rach, but could you get a ride home? I'm wanted ASAP for a quick meeting."

Rachel nodded. "Thanks for taking me shopping and stuff."

Patrice smiled. "Don't worry so much. You're a shoo-in." She waved at me. "See you, Serena. I'll text you later, okay?"

I smiled and she whisked out in a flash of dark hair and designer perfume. Her parents must have serious bankroll.

Rachel squealed and flopped down onto my covered bed. "I knew it! She *is* going to ask you."

I grinned at her excitement. "Ask me what?"

Rachel sat up. "To be in the sorority," she whispered. She

hopped off the bed and tiptoed to the door. "Okay, you can't tell a soul that I told you, okay? If they invite you to join, they will tell you all about it and you have to act like you don't know. Promise?"

Rachel's eyes bored into mine and I resisted the urge to cross my heart and hope to die. "I promise."

"Okay, 'cause I've been waiting my whole life to be in the sorority and I don't want to blow it. The sorority has been around forever. Like thirty-five years or something. Basically, it's a secret club for girls. Only the girls with the most potential are able to join."

I raised an eyebrow. "Potential?"

"Yeah, to be popular, but it doesn't end there. Membership in the sorority can make your social life for years to come. If there's a sorority girl already going to the college you are about to go to, then it's her job to help you get into the best sorority there. It can even help if you do business. One former sorority woman went into real estate and now owns her own firm because of sorority referrals."

"Why is it such a secret?"

Rachel snorted. "Exclusive organizations are banned from the school. They cracked down after some girls got hurt a few years back. So we just went underground."

"We?"

Rachel blushed. "My mom was in the sorority, so they have to at least give me a chance. Plus, Patrice and I have been friends for a long time. As long as I make it through initiation week, I'm in."

That didn't sound good. "What do they do to you?"

"Humiliate us. Find the most embarrassing things they can think of and throw them at us. Last year Patrice and Sonya had to go to the mall with tampons in their hair like curlers. It was hysterical."

I noticed she wasn't laughing and the shadows in her blue eyes betrayed her worry. "Is it really worth it? I mean, do you get to do anything?"

"They have the best parties ever, and you get to go on a trip to Florida for spring break. It's totally worth it."

Was a week of humiliation worth a Florida sunburn? I wasn't sure. "So how do you get to be in the sorority?"

"The seniors elect a nominating committee made up of the top junior girls. Their job is to come up with a list of desirable sophomores. That's what Sonya and Patrice are doing. That's why they are hanging out with us so much. After the seniors approve the list, the fun begins. For them. Not for us."

"What about the freshmen? Aren't any freshman girls nominated?"

Rachel shook her head. "Nope. We get to choose them next year. The theory is that we would know the incoming girls better 'cause we went to school with them longer." She bounced up and down on the bed. "It would be so awesome if you could be in the sorority with us. It'll be a blast."

"Humiliation always is," I said dryly.

"No, you don't understand. Once you're in, you are *in*. A total It girl. Forever."

I smiled at her, but my stomach churned. Trouble was, I'm not sure I'm It-girl material.

Five

Mom and I worked like maniacs all weekend, and by the time Sunday evening rolled around, most of the painting was finished. The carpeting people were coming later in the week to lay the new carpet, and I could see the end in sight. All of my belongings had been pulled out into the hall. I was pretty tired of living out of a box, but the results would be *so* worth it.

I'd curled up on the couch with a manga. I loved escaping into really good Japanese mangas because the art form was so cool and the language, mostly translated from Japanese, was easy and fun. My body ached from all the work on the bedroom and I wanted to kick back.

A tap on the shoulder made me jump.

"Come on, sweetheart, we're heading up to Shirley and Alan's. Your dad has to fix Alan's computer so they can network back and forth. Or something like that."

The last thing I wanted to do was face Miller. "Can't I just stay home?"

"Nope, you can go." Mom's voice sounded firm and clear as a bell. "You can apologize and make nice. He did a lot of work yesterday and you should be grateful." Her face softened. "Don't feel bad. I'm sure Miller won't hold a thoughtless comment against you."

Poor Mom. Talk about clueless. Of course, she didn't know how Miller felt about the preps, nor had she heard Patrice's remark.

I grumbled but went. No use fighting Mom's newfound zest for community and family.

My cousins Zach and Nate greeted me at the door like returning royalty. Okay, that was pretty cool. They wriggled around me like puppies, minus the wagging tails and tongues hanging out.

"Miller's out at the kennels if you'd like to go say hi."

Now why would Aunt Shirley think that? But Mom flashed me *the look*. Peacemaking time.

The boys escorted me to the barn, and though I had a hard time deciphering their excited high-pitched boy squeals, it didn't seem to matter. I nodded and smiled as if I heard and understood all of it. That seemed to satisfy them.

Miller was in with one of the animals when we got there. The boys told me the old golden-retriever cross was named Arnold. Arnold's rapturous moans were audible even to me as Miller rubbed his back.

Miller looked up and nodded when I entered, then returned his attention to Arnold.

Zach and Nate wandered around the room feeding the other dogs their treats. Then they zoomed off into the little-dog room.

"He looks happy," I ventured when Miller said nothing.

"He knows who his friends are. Don't ya, Arnold, old boy?"

I fidgeted against the kennel. Was there a hidden meaning in that? "Look, Miller, I'm sorry about yesterday, I didn't mean . . . "

He stopped scratching Arnold's back and his mouth twisted into an ironic smile. "It's like we're always apologizing to each other. Why don't we start over?"

"Start over?"

He opened the kennel door and held out his hand. "Hi, my name is Miller. Nice to meet you."

I giggled and shook his hand, no longer surprised by the electrical current that ran through my body every time I touched him. A girl could get used to feeling like that. "Nice to meet you, too. My name is Serena. I just started at the school last week and it totally sucked! I dumped my lunch on some poor guy, made some friends, and made some enemies. Oh, and I was almost run down in the road the other day by a football player with a Dale Earnhardt Jr. complex."

Miller's smile morphed into a scowl. "What? Who almost ran you down? When?"

His concern warmed me. See, he did like me. "The other day. It was stupid. I wasn't watching where I was going. No big deal, really." My stomach flipped, remembering how sick I'd felt afterward.

"You tell me if anything like that happens again, okay? Promise?"

Miller's stormy eyes sent shivers down my back and I nodded, surprised by his intensity. I suddenly felt shy, something that rarely happened with guys. I guess I was going to have to accept the fact that nothing was normal around this one. I looked away.

"Hey, twerps!" Miller called into the next room. He turned back to me. "We have to keep an eye on them in here. They might let the dogs out just for fun."

I laughed as the boys scampered in.

"Wanna help Serena and me take the dogs for a walk before it gets dark?"

In answer they grabbed a tangle of leashes and collars off the wall.

I laughed at their eagerness. "I take that as a yes."

Again I marveled at Miller's gentleness as he collared an excited Brutus and a slim gray and white Australian-shepherd mix called Laurie. Brutus was large and exuberant, but dainty, well-mannered Laurie ignored all of his efforts to get her excited.

The well-worn trail we walked circled around the farm and into the woods before winding its way back to the barn.

The boys ran in front of us, enjoying the bright autumn evening.

"So where are you going to college?" I asked.

Miller shrugged. "Not sure. I've been sending out applications. I'm going to have to have a job, and I haven't decided whether it would be cheaper to live on campus or go in with some other guys and rent a house. I did well on my PSATs last year, so I'll get a merit scholarship, but I want to save enough of my money so that I can open up my own business if I want."

"Do you get good grades?" I asked.

Miller looked sheepish. "I'm actually on the honor roll. I have a 4.0."

My mouth fell open. I barely pulled above average except in math. That language thing again. But a 4.0? Sullen, brooding Miller?

He laughed. "Don't look so shocked."

"No, I'm not. I'm sure you're very smart. I just didn't—"

"Didn't expect it?" He grinned and yanked on Brutus's leash as the dog tried to take Laurie's head gently into his mouth.

"Well, no," I admitted. "I mean, I know you're smart—I just thought you'd be more of a rebel."

He kept his eyes fixed on Brutus but spoke loudly enough for me to hear. "I promised my mom. She was so worried about me and I didn't want her to think about anything but getting better, so I promised her I would keep my grades up."

Uh-huh. I wasn't touching that one. "So where's your dad?" I asked instead.

Miller's lip curled and his pace increased. "He left when I was five. Haven't heard from him since. Mom sent a letter to his parents when she was diagnosed, but we never heard from them, either."

My heart ached, but I didn't have time to express it before Miller stopped short, causing a surprised Brutus to sit back on his haunches.

"Look, I'm sick of everyone feeling sorry for me," Miller said. "I don't need you feeling sorry for me, too. I'm fine."

I heard that. I also understood. "Hey, I get it. Trust me."

He looked at me for a long moment, his eyes searching. Finally he grinned. "Yeah, I guess you do."

We walked in silence for a few more minutes. Then I thought of something. Maybe he could give me more info on the sorority.

"Hey, have you ever heard of a secret sorority for girls?"

He laughed and my heart pounded at the sound. I could fall in love with a guy like this. The surprise of that thought almost made me stop in my tracks, but I forced myself to continue walking.

"It's not really that much of a secret. Only from the administration. Some of your friends are in it, or are going to be. I've heard the initiation can be pretty rough."

I swallowed. "Like how?"

"They've honed humiliation into an art form."

I digested that. I wasn't so good with humiliation. I'd been humiliated too many times in my life by mis-understanding people or not being able to say something correctly to sign on for more. But if it would make me some friends . . .

"They all act like it's such a big deal," he continued, his voice edged with bitterness. "They don't know what really matters."

"What do you mean?"

He stopped and looked at me, his dark eyes unreadable. "Popularity isn't the most important thing in the world. Flipping your hair around and having flat abs won't give you a fulfilling life."

I knew what he was saying was really important and mature, but I couldn't get past his mouth. I stared at it and imagined him kissing me. Just kissing me till I couldn't think. Or what if I kissed him? It's not like I'd never been the aggressor. Why did he almost paralyze me? I leaned toward him, my eyes locked with his. He reached up and ran his finger over my bottom lip. My lips parted slightly and my heart pounded. *Do it!*

"We should get the dogs in," he said, staring at my mouth. "And the kids. We can finish our conversation later."

I swallowed and nodded. Tingles reached from my toes all the way to my hairline. *Later.*

Too bad he wouldn't talk to me the next day.

I went to school on a cloud of happiness and possibilities.

He liked me. He cared about what happened to me. I had friends. My bedroom ranked up there in the top fifty coolest rooms in the world.

Then I ran into Miller going into American history.

"Hi there!" I gave him a vivacious smile. One that would melt all his schooltime angst. One that would make him realize we could be so much more than friends.

And he nodded and walked to his seat without a single backward glance.

What the hell was his problem, anyway? I glared at him several times during class. He rarely spoke except when the teacher asked him a question. He sat there looking brooding and superior. What crap.

I fumed all during American history. I was so pissed off, I'd walked halfway to the cafeteria before I realized I'd left my history book on the desk.

"I'll catch up to you in a minute," I told Rachel, who nodded and continued on.

I hurried back to the classroom, but slowed when I saw Ms. Fisher talking to another teacher. I'd avoided Ms. Fisher ever since the whole sign-language thing and Ms. Fisher seemed to avoid me, too. I saw what they were talking about even from down the hall.

"Wait till the kids get a load of the pop quiz I'm giving them tomorrow," Ms. Fisher said to the other teacher. "No one will expect it the second week of school."

The other teacher laughed. "You are so bad, Nancy."

Ms. Fisher opened her mouth to say something but stopped when she saw me.

"I forgot something," I said.

"Good thing you got here before I locked up for lunch," Ms. Fisher said.

I nodded and darted into the classroom.

"Thanks," I said on my way out.

The girls were in deep conversation when I finally made it to the table with my lunch. I hesitated at joining them without an invitation but Rachel waved her hand.

I sat down but they all ignored me as they huddled around Sonya, who was in the middle of a story. Sonya raised her eyebrows at me as if I didn't have a right to be there. She spoke too softly for me to hear and her face was turned away from me, so I couldn't even read her lips. I waited for some kind of acknowledgment from someone else, but when none came, I shrugged my shoulders.

"I guess no one wants to hear what I lip-read today." I hadn't even counted to three before Patrice turned to me, excitement etched on her face.

"What?"

"Ohhh, juicy gossip," Kelly said.

Sonya glared and Rachel scooted closer.

Much better.

I looked at Patrice. "You take American history in the class before Rachel and me, right?"

Patrice nodded. "Kelly, Sonya, and I all do."

I twisted open my water and took a swig, enjoying their impatience. "Well, I don't know about you all, but I am going to be up late studying tonight." I paused and took another long, slow drink. I really should take up drama. "Because Ms. Fisher is giving us a pop quiz tomorrow."

Patrice's mouth fell open. "You're amazing. My parents will kill me if I bring home a single bad grade this year."

Rachel slung an arm around me and gave me a squeeze. "Incredible. It's like having our own oracle!"

Suddenly Patrice reached out and grabbed my arm. "There's Scott and Craig. Quick—what are they saying?"

I looked and then laughed. "They're not even facing me. I read lips, not minds."

Patrice slumped in her chair. "Oh."

My stomach turned. Maybe she wouldn't invite me to her party if I didn't find out something. Worried, I glanced back at the guys. They turned toward me and I focused on their lips.

"Hold on," Scott was saying. "I'm going to ask Patrice to the dance before somebody else does."

I hit Patrice and waved a hand at Scott sauntering toward us. "Get ready," I whispered. "He's about to ask you to the dance."

Patrice gave me an incredulous look before joining Scott, who'd indicated he wanted to talk to her.

"Oh, oh, see if you can see what he's saying to her," Kelly said.

"Oh, I couldn't do that." I pursed my lips and widened

my eyes. The picture of innocence. "That would be eaves-dropping."

They all cracked up except for Sonya, who scowled at Patrice and Scott.

A few moments later Patrice came over and hugged me. "I love you!" She sat down, her eyes alight. "We're gonna have a blast at my homecoming party."

I smiled up at Patrice, but my smile faded when I caught Sonya's frozen glare. I squirmed. I hated being on somebody's hit list.

Sonya widened her eyes. "Patrice? Do you really think that's a good idea? I thought it was going to be an *exclusive* party."

Kayla nodded her head in agreement. As if she ever disagreed with Sonya. No wonder I thought of her as the evil twin. "She's right. That's what I thought, too."

Yep, California was definitely missing a beach bimbo.

Patrice and Sonya glared at each other. The air was suddenly so thick with animosity, you could almost see it flowing between them in a stream.

"Are you telling me who I can and can't invite to my own party?" Patrice's voice dripped with ice.

"No, but don't you think you should clear it with Annie and Meredith?" Sonya's voice was just as cold.

Patrice's pretty lips curved into a frigid smile. "I already have."

Sonya's eyes flashed, but she visibly controlled herself.

"That's fine, then. That's all I wanted to know."

I guess Patrice won that little exchange.

I saw Miller across the room. This might be a good time to make my exit.

I picked up my tray of half-eaten food. "Sorry, guys, I have to run, but I will let you know if I come up with any more good dirt!"

I hurried to dump my tray and tried to catch up with Miller, who had headed down the hall. He turned the corner and I followed him into the dinky school library.

The scent of old books assaulted my nose as I tried to see where he had gone. Everything about the library looked patched and worn, including the librarian behind the desk. I used to love the library at my old school. It hadn't mattered that I wasn't much of a reader. The computers and the vast anime collection kept me going back even though the books themselves weren't all that enticing. I'd learned right off the bat this library wasn't even on the same level. Only one ancient computer and no mangas whatsoever. The librarian had given me a couple of old *Star Wars* books when I'd asked about it.

I finally saw Miller down the nonfiction aisle and I snuck up behind him.

"I think I'm going to have to start calling you Moody Miller."

He jumped and whirled around. "What are you doing here?"

He didn't look happy, but neither was I. "I go to school here. Duh."

"I meant, what are you doing in the library? Aren't your friends waiting for you?"

I blinked. "No, I wanted to talk to you."

The muscles in his face relaxed. "I'm looking up books on the SATs. If I can ace them, I may be able to get a full ride somewhere."

"So what's that one?"

He turned the book over and I read the title.

"*Acing the SATs*. Won't that help?"

"It's from 1994."

"Oh." We both looked at the dilapidated, dog-eared book in his hands and started laughing. "Yeah, I don't think that will be much help. Isn't there a public library around here?"

"Yeah, I'll try that next."

I bit my lip before speaking again. "Would you like to go after school? I could help you look."

I held my breath, waiting for his response.

"I guess we could," he said. "I have to get home pretty fast after that, though. I have to help with the critters."

"The boys or the dogs?" I teased.

"Both!"

We grinned at each other and agreed to meet at the front door of the school after the bell.

I wanted to tell Miller, "See, that wasn't so difficult." I

just wished I knew why he treated me like I had the plague whenever we were at school.

The rest of the afternoon passed in a happy haze until Patrice caught up with me on my way out the door.

"Where are you off to in such a hurry? I wanted to invite you out for some food and a lip-reading session. Jerry's is the best for juicy gossip. Plus, I have something important I wanted to talk to you about."

Oh gawd, would she hate me if I said I couldn't go? And what did she want to talk to me about? The sorority? "Oh, uh, I already made plans."

"Really? Who with?" The chill in Patrice's voice made a blizzard look cozy. Chick was scary.

I checked to see if Miller weas around. "I actually made plans with Miller. We're going up to work in my aunt's kennels."

"Oh, a family gig. Gotcha. Can't you get out of it though? I mean, I know Miller is practically family, but I wouldn't make a practice of hanging out with him. He's kind of rough, and you don't want that kind of reputation, do you?" Patrice flashed a glowing smile.

My heart leaped in my chest. What was she saying? I couldn't be a part of the sorority *and* have a relationship with Miller? I wished I had the guts to tell her that no one could run my life and I would see who I wanted to. But a flash of what she was offering ran through my head—a sense of belonging, of being popular, not to mention how happy and relieved my mom would be to see me in the A-list crowd. It might actually tone down the mother hover.

Someone tapped me on the shoulder and I turned. "You ready to go?"

Miller stood behind me, his eyes flat and unreadable.

I swallowed against the lump in my throat, hating myself. "I'm so sorry. I totally forgot that I'd made plans with Patrice this afternoon. Maybe tomorrow?"

My eyes pleaded with him to understand.

He gave me a small, sad smile. "Sure, no problem."

I turned and hurried down the stairs. Tears stung my eyes.

Patrice caught up with me and linked my arm in hers. "This is going to be so fun!"

I nodded, not trusting my voice. Fun, huh? So far, not so much.

Six

"Okay, so what do you want me to do?"

Patrice, Rachel, and Sonya sat around the booth in all their A-list glory. Sonya looked pinched to be sitting with me, but then again Sonya always looked pinched.

Patrice ran her fingers through her silky dark hair and flashed me a wolf's grin. "Time to go deep cover! I've been trying to figure out a way we can use your lipreading ability to the max. It's hard to know when someone's going to say something juicy. You kind of have to luck into it, like you did today with the pop quiz."

I nodded and chewed on my thumbnail. I wished Patrice would get to the point.

Rachel yawned. "So?"

"So, I figure we need to get Serena in a place where she can hear all the gossip, all the dirt. And where would that be?"

"Oh, come on, just tell us," Rachel said. "I'm exhausted and I have to stay up late tonight studying for the test." She flashed me a grateful smile and I grinned at her.

"The office!" Patrice beamed.

My eyes widened. "The what?"

"The office," Patrice repeated louder.

I waved my hand. "No, I heard you the first time—I just don't get it."

"You know, Patrice, I think you might be on to something," Rachel said slowly. "Everything happens in the office. Kids are sent there when they're in trouble, policies are changed there, attendance, meetings . . . everything."

Patrice nodded. "Exactly. I'm a genius."

"I think it's a dumb idea," Sonya muttered.

"That's just because you didn't think of it first," snapped Patrice. "I think it's brilliant. Besides, think about how much it could help us." Patrice blinked her eyes at Sonya, who rolled hers.

I shuffled my feet. *Diabolical* was more like it. How was I supposed to get out of this? "I don't know anything about working in an office."

Patrice flashed me another wicked grin. "That's the beauty of it. You don't have to. What are you taking as an elective?"

"Art, but my schedule's all set."

"Do you like it?" she asked.

I shook my head. "Not really."

"Then here's what you do. You go tell the guidance counselor that it's not working out for you for whatever reason. That you're allergic to art or something. Then tell him you want to work in the office instead. They always allow a few select students to work in there each semester and get credit for it. You're a shoo-in."

I swallowed. "Why's that? What if they don't let me?"

Patrice put her arm around my shoulder. "'Cause you're a new student and you're deaf. They'll be falling all over them-selves to make you happy. Being deaf is your ticket in!"

I swallowed to keep from gagging. After years of trying to fit in, of minimizing my deafness so I'd be considered normal, Patrice wanted me to use it to get special privileges.

Rachel must have seen the look on my face. "Only if you want to. But it would be fun."

Patrice laughed and gave me a squeeze before letting go of me. "Of course she wants to! She's our friend; she's one of us now. Oh, come on, it'll be awesome."

"Don't make her. She obviously doesn't want to," Sonya said.

I glanced at Sonya, suddenly suspicious. *So why don't you want me in the office?*

Rachel and Patrice smiled at me with a mixture of excitement and daring. Patrice's words—*she's one of us now*—echoed though my mind. "I'll do it," I said with a sigh.

Patrice gave an excited squeal. "Fabulous! Talk to the guidance counselor tomorrow, okay? And let's keep this to ourselves. The more people who know what we're doing, the better our chances at getting caught."

I almost groaned out loud. I hadn't even thought of that. Maybe fitting in wasn't all it was cracked up to be.

Sonya shrugged. "Look, you do whatever you want to. I personally don't think it's that much of an asset for us." She scooted out of the booth and moved to a table filled with seniors.

Patrice frowned and watched her go. She turned back to Rachel and me. "Rachel can you give us a minute? Thanks, hon."

Rachel, barely hid her smile as she wandered off to talk to friends.

Patrice leaned toward me and folded her hands on the table, all business. "Serena, I like you. You're gutsy and I think the way you read lips is totally awesome. I believe we can help each other out."

My eyes narrowed. "I'm already spying—sorry, working—for you in the office. How else can I help you?"

"I'll tell you, but first I have to know that what I'm about to tell you isn't going any further, okay? Promise?"

I gulped. "Promise."

"Okay. I belong to a very exclusive secret sorority. No one knows about it. Well, obviously people know about it, but we try to keep it on the down-low. Sonya and I are both up for president during our senior year. And I need your help to make sure I get it."

I was so not expecting that. "What can I do?"

"See if you can get any dirt on her by keeping your ear to the ground." She giggled at her own joke.

I gave her a wan smile.

"No, really—I want you to do some covert lip-reading and see if you can't find out anything that might discredit her."

She hadn't said a word about asking me to join and I was tempted to tell her to forget it, but then she grabbed the proverbial carrot in her hand and dangled it in front of me.

"Also, I think there just might be a place for you in the sorority. Your skills could come in *verrry* handy. I have to turn in the list of prospective members next week, and I think your name might be included. That is, if you want it to be."

She leaned back and took a sip from her soda.

My heart thudded against my ribs. Here it was. Did I really want to? I'd never imagined really belonging to anything like that.

I'd never had the *chance*.

Sure, she was using me. I wasn't stupid. The question was, would I let her? How important was fitting in? I glanced around the restaurant at the kids hanging out. Rachel stood by the door talking to Kayla and Kelly who had just walked in. Kelly waved and Rachel turned and gave me the thumbs-up with a wide grin.

Suddenly I knew I wanted it more than anything in the world. "Of course I want to!"

Patrice beamed. "Fabulous! Let's get the others over here and celebrate."

I nodded. This was great, right? So how come I felt like I'd just sold my soul to the devil?

By the time I hit third period the next day, I had a new schedule in my hot little hand. Instead of ending my days with mind-numbing art, I'd be making copies and filing. Oh, goody.

Rachel dropped a note over my shoulder.

"Did you do it?"

I turned my head and nodded, but didn't have time to say anything because Ms. Fisher announced the pop quiz with glee.

I wasn't the only one prepared. While most of the class looked shell-shocked, others looked smug. Word had obviously gotten around. Patrice was right to keep Operation Read My Lips a secret. Of course, that included Sonya, and I didn't trust her for squat.

I peeked over at Miller, busily writing on the sheet of paper Ms. Fisher had handed out. Maybe I should have told him. But no. Something told me he wouldn't approve of my lip-spying. I sighed and turned to my own work. I hated history. I reviewed all the questions on the quiz. No problemo. Good thing I'd read through the chapters last night.

I answered the questions easily and turned my paper in. The teacher seemed suspicious of how quickly some of her students finished the quiz.

"If you're done, you can be dismissed early for lunch," she said, studying the growing pile of papers with a puzzled frown.

"So you got in?" Rachel asked when we left the room.

"Yep. Operation Read My Lips is in full swing."

Rachel giggled. "This is gonna be so much fun. I'm so excited Patrice wants you to be a part of the sorority. We get to go through initiation week together."

Oh goody, again. "When exactly is this big initiation week, anyway?"

Rachel's forehead wrinkled. "Week after next."

"Can't wait. Look, I'll catch up to you in a minute. I want to talk to someone."

Rachel tossed her blond hair and tilted her head. "And exactly who would that be? Some dark-haired rebel without a cause?"

I pushed her toward the cafeteria. "Go on!"

I didn't mind Rachel knowing. As long as she didn't say anything to Patrice.

I fidgeted outside the door, trying not to think about this afternoon's covert ops. What had I gotten myself into?

The door opened and another student came out, followed by Miller.

"How did you do?" I asked.

"Not bad, considering I didn't know it was coming. How about you?"

I shrugged. "I don't know. I guess I'll have to wait and see." Totally time for a subject change. "Did you want some help at the kennels tonight?"

His shoulders twitched. "I don't know. If you want to."

"But do *you* want me to?" I persisted.

His eyes darted down the hallway. "Sure, that would be great," he said absently.

I was tired of this bullshit. Just a couple nights ago we had come inches from kissing and now he was giving me the brush-off? I ignored the little voice inside me that reminded me that I had brushed him off, too. I just wanted to know if he liked me or not. That wasn't too much to ask, was it? I took a deep breath. "Okay, look, maybe I'm getting my signals crossed, but I thought that we had, I dunno, sort of a moment the other night. Was it a moment or am I delusional?"

His eyes softened. "It was a moment."

"Okay," I said, somewhat mollified. "I'll have my mom drive me over this evening."

"I could just take you after school."

I looked down at the floor. "Actually, I have—"

"Plans," he finished for me, his voice distant again. "Okay, this evening, then."

And without another word he turned and left me standing alone in the hallway.

Jerk.

· · ·

"AND THE *B*s GO WHERE THE *B*s ARE!" Mrs. Watson smiled at me, causing her eyes to disappear into her wrinkles.

What? Did she think I was an idiot 'cause I was deaf?

"Thank you. I think I can do it now," I told her.

"GOOD! GOOD! JUST CALL ME IF YOU HAVE ANY QUESTIONS!"

I wished Mrs. Watson would quit yelling. Not only did it cause my hearing aids to squeak, but it made her mouth move funny so I could barely read her lips. I turned to the stack of files, but Mrs. Watson wasn't finished with me yet.

"OH, AND SERENA, EVERYTHING THAT HAP-PENS IN THIS OFFICE IS CONFIDENTIAL AND STAYS IN THE OFFICE! IF YOU ARE CAUGHT VIOLATING THAT RULE, YOU LOSE THE CREDIT AND WILL BE IMMEDIATELY SUSPENDED. BUT I'M SURE THAT WON'T BE A PROBLEM!"

I shook my head, but my heart thudded against my chest. Suspension? Freaking great.

I filed until my fingers were numb. Were they still living in the dark ages? Hadn't anyone in this school ever heard of a computer? I glanced up at the mammoth filing cabinets filling the room. Obviously not.

While alphabetizing paperwork, I kept an eye out for any-thing interesting. So far, nothing. If this was the happening place in school, I'd hate to be stuck in the boring part. Two kids went home sick and the PE teacher came in with a kid who refused to run laps. Teachers and administrators came and went, but no one said anything worth repeating. Not that I'd be able to tell much with my head stuck in the *M*s.

I bent to the *N*s.

"SERENA!"

I jumped, slamming my head on the file drawer above.

"OH, HONEY, ARE YOU OKAY?"

I clenched my teeth and nodded.

"GOOD! WOULD YOU LIKE TO RUN THESE BACK TO MR. LUTZ?" She handed me some papers. "IT'S THE SECOND DOOR TO THE RIGHT AND IT SAYS 'DEAN OF STUDENTS' ON IT."

Mrs. Watson gave me another scrunchy smile before I turned and made my way back to the dean's office.

The office, like most in the school, had a large glass window in the wall to keep counselors and administrators from perving on the students. Mr. Lutz stood with another man, who handed him something that he slipped into his pocket. The way it had been done caught my attention. I slowed and focused on their lips.

"For God's sake, don't tell anyone," Mr. Lutz was saying. "My wife would kill me, and my reputation would be ruined."

The other man said something, but I couldn't catch it.

"Because sometimes you just need a cigarette, you know?"

I backed up down the hall and scurried back to Mrs. Watson. "Which room is Mr. Lutz's?"

"DON'T WORRY ABOUT IT. I HAVE TO GO BACK THERE ANYWAY. YOU CAN GO BACK TO FILING."

I did as I was told, but my mind whirled. Why would getting caught smoking ruin his reputation?

The bell rang just above my head and I jumped again. I'd have to remember to turn my aids down when I got here or office work would finish off the hearing I had left.

Rachel met me at the office door. "So did you get anything?"

I laughed. "Yeah. Paper cuts."

"Poor baby. Patrice is waiting outside to give us a lift. We're gonna stop at Jerry's on the way home. Can you?"

I nodded. "Patrice told me about it yesterday when she dropped me off. I already cleared it with the mother figure. She was thrilled."

Rachel glanced at me, questions in her eyes.

I laughed. "She wants me to be happy here."

"Got it. My mom's the same way."

Rachel linked her arm in mine and we dashed down the stairs to where Patrice waited impatiently.

Patrice drove like a maniac all the way to Jerry's. Did everyone drive like that here? Was it something in the water? The tunes were cranked, so I settled back into the seat and shut my eyes.

Patrice had a hard time finding a parking spot. "This place is always packed," Rachel complained after Patrice turned the car and the music off.

Patrice laughed and slammed her door shut. "That's because it's the only place in town that'll put up with us."

"Oh, I almost forgot," Patrice said as we walked through the parking lot. "The party is at eight this Friday night. I can't pick you up, 'cause I have to be there, but Rachel said she can."

The party was really going to happen and I was still invited! Okay, I felt a little lame for being so excited . . . but I didn't care!

Stay cool. "Sure. Sounds great."

"Awesome! Oh, and my parents said I could have it, so it's not like it's on the DL or anything. Just in case your 'rents wanna know."

Hmm, my parents were gonna want to know. Mom would probably insist on checking the place for alcohol before she'd let me go. Hell, she'd probably bring in drug-sniffing dogs. Oh, well. I'd cross that bridge later. Much, much later.

Most of the booths were taken when we got inside, but Sonya already had one so we joined her. Great.

We ordered a side of fries and a plate of nachos to share, then they all turned to me.

Patrice leaned closer. "So what's the dirt? Anything juicy happen?"

"Oh my God, Patrice! Get a life!" Sonya tapped her fingers and looked bored, but I could see interest in the bright spark of her eyes.

Either that or she was channeling Satan.

I gave my friends an accusatory glare. "First off, I think I should be charging for this. Not one of you warned me about Mrs. Watson. And I thought we were friends."

Rachel and Patrice giggled. "Sorry—did you get *loved* to death?" Rachel asked.

"Just about. Also, did you guys know that I could get suspended for telling you anything that goes on there?"

Sonya smirked. "She didn't find anything out," she told the other girls.

Disappointment broke on Patrice's face. "Really?"

So much for anyone being concerned about my academic future. "No, actually I did, but I don't know how big of a deal it is."

Patrice took a sip from her soda. "Tell us and we'll decide."

I shrugged. "Okay. I was walking toward the hall and I saw some teacher—"

"Who was it?" Sonya asked.

"I don't know. Just some guy."

"Shut up, Sonya. Let her talk," Patrice said.

"Anyway," I continued, "the guy handed Mr. Lutz something. I couldn't see what it was, but they were all secretive-like, so I read their lips."

Rachel was all ears. "What were they saying?"

The waitress brought our food, but no one touched it.

"Let's see. Mr. Lutz said not to tell anyone because his wife would kill him and it would ruin his reputation."

I paused. All around us orders were being served, kids

were eating and table hopping, but the girls at my table were so focused on me, they were barely breathing.

I liked that.

"He said, 'because sometimes you just need a cigarette.'"

I leaned back, judging their reactions. Rachel gasped and put her hand over her mouth. Patrice squealed, and even Sonya bounced in her seat. Then the three of them laughed till their eyes were streaming. Sonya actually had mascara running down her face.

I watched them with a little frown. "I must be missing something."

The girls calmed down and wiped their eyes.

Rachel held her stomach. "Oh, God, that's the hardest I've laughed in, like, forever."

Patrice nodded and bit into a fry. "Me too. That was wicked funny," she said with her mouth full.

I plucked a cheesy chip from the pile of nachos. "Okay, who wants to fill in the new girl?"

"You've seen those antismoking posters in the hallways right?" Rachel asked.

I nodded. "Yeah, the school is practically wallpapered with them."

"They were put there by No-Butts Lutz himself," Sonya said, which sent the girls back into hysterical laughter.

"What?"

Patrice tried to control herself. "Mr. Lutz was a chain-smoker since he was, like, born. After he quit last spring, he went on an anticigarette rampage in the school, including lectures, the posters, and unannounced locker searches."

"It was like a witch hunt for the smokers of the school," Rachel said, dipping a fry into Thousand Island. "Caused a lot of controversy. So we started calling him No-Butts Lutz 'cause his antismoking campaign was called No More Butts."

I laughed and covered my mouth with my hand. "Oh my gawd. That's awful. So No-Butts Lutz is smoking again."

"I guess so," Patrice said.

Poor guy. No wonder he was terrified of being caught. "So what are you going to do?"

Patrice shrugged. "I don't know. Nothing right now. They didn't see you, did they?"

"No—they have no idea I was even there."

"You're good," Rachel congratulated me.

So how come I felt so guilty?

Just then Miller walked through the door. I turned away, my eyes darting over to the take-out counter.

"I think we should keep this to ourselves," Rachel said. "It wouldn't help us in any way to share it, and it would hurt him a lot. And he's not that bad of a dean."

"No, he's just another hypocrite," Sonya said.

I looked back up to where Miller waited for his order. He glanced over, and for a moment our eyes locked before I turned my head and slouched down in my seat.

"But then again," Sonya said, staring from me to Miller, "maybe we're all hypocrites in one way or another."

Seven

Patrice dropped me off in front of my house, and I rushed up the walkway. I had to get to the kennels for some damage control.

"Mom?" I called, bursting through the door. "Are you around?"

The house was silent, but that didn't mean anything. I wouldn't hear Mom calling from upstairs anyway. I dumped my backpack in the foyer and searched the house. Then I peered down into the basement.

"Dad?"

"I'm down here, sweetie."

I almost turned to leave him alone but decided not to. I hadn't seen much of him since he and Uncle Alan started their consulting business.

"Do you know where Mom is?" I asked, coming down the steps.

"She ran to the hardware store for something for our room. Some doohickey. I don't know what."

I laughed. Mom could fix anything. Dad couldn't hammer a nail.

"She did a nice job down here, didn't she?" I said.

We looked around the basement, which Mom had turned from a dank haven for spiders into a bright, professional work space using paint and wainscoting.

"Yeah, she did. Wait till she starts freelancing. She's going to take this town by storm."

Mom had had a busy interior-decorating business back home that she had loved. I suddenly wondered why we'd moved. I'd never heard Dad complaining about his job, and Mom had loved hers. We'd had a nice home and everything.

"Dad, can I ask you a question?"

He swiveled his chair toward me. "Sounds serious. What's up?"

"Why did we move? I know you said it was because you wanted to be closer to family and wanted to start a business with Uncle Alan. But was that really why?"

He looked at me, his eyes serious. "That was definitely part of the reason we moved, but you were a big part of the equation."

I wasn't surprised. I knew more had to be going on than they'd let on. "Me? Why? I liked my own school okay."

"Yes, but you weren't thriving there. You were going through the motions. We knew if you were to survive and thrive in the world, you would need more. A sense of community."

I snorted. "So you moved me to the boondocks?"

Dad laughed. "I'd hardly call this the boondocks. But you have family here. And it's easier to find a sense of belonging in a small town. At least, we hope so. We know how tough it is being an oral deaf teenager. You had a hard time fitting in with the kids in your old school, and most of your deaf peers spoke sign language, so you didn't really fit in there, either."

"So basically you raised a freak," I teased, but my stomach tightened.

Dad winked. "No, not a freak, but definitely a weirdo. Maybe we should have kept signing with you, but when you stopped . . ." He shrugged. "You didn't seem to need it."

I shook my head. "I don't really remember that."

"We figured that if you could find your place here, you would have a sense of belonging no matter where you decided to go or what you decided to do."

I nodded. "That makes sense, but you forgot something."

"What's that?"

"What if moving here is a total disaster? You have a backup plan?"

He shrugged. "Not really. Your mom and I have always liked living life on the edge."

I laughed at the corny face he made and I moved to go upstairs. "Dad, do me a favor. Never make that face in public, okay?"

"Sure."

He went back to his computer and I darted upstairs.

Mom was back by the time I got to the living room.

"Mom, can you take me up to Aunt Shirley's? I want to help out in the kennels." *And spend more time with Miller.* Somewhere safe where Patrice couldn't bust us. That is, if he was still talking to me after ignoring him at Jerry's.

Mom set the bag she was holding in her arms down onto the kitchen counter. "Before or after dinner?"

"Before. Like right now?"

"Sure, let me get my keys."

Soon after we pulled up in front of the kennels. Mom eyed the dogs hopping around the car with distrust. "You be careful, okay? And give everyone my best. Call me when you want to come home."

Aunt Shirley's own dogs nosed my legs in delirious joy at having a visitor. I went directly to the kennels, figuring that Miller would probably be working already.

I let my eyes adjust to the dimness of the barn and went in search of Miller. He wasn't in with the big dogs or the little dogs, so I tiptoed back to where they kept the fresh hay and other supplies. Maybe I could sneak up on him.

I peered around the adge of the door and my breath caught in my throat. He was in there, all right. Naked from the waist up. His shirt hung on a peg a few feet from me. I didn't know such a slender guy could be so built. But as he stacked hay, muscles rippled in his arms and chest.

I tried to tell him I was there, but my lips were suddenly dry. My arms and legs froze. and I could no more take a step into that room than I could fly. I tried to conjure up visions of my old skater friends riding their boards without shirts, but the sight of them had never paralyzed me like this.

So I squeaked. I actually meant to clear my throat, but squeaked instead. Like a baby bird on its deathbed.

He looked up and heat rose in my face.

"Hey." He casually walked over next to me, pulled his shirt off the peg, and slipped it on. He didn't button it up, though, so it hung open in the front.

Oh, goody. Now he was only part naked. The problem was, the open shirt only worked to showcase his abs and chest, and they were so fine, I wanted to—

"Serena?" His brows knit together, puzzled, and his eyes sought mine. When our eyes met, they caught and locked. His eyes darkened and I wondered what they had seen in mine to make them change. Hormones? Phero-mones? Must have been something, because his scent enveloped me as he leaned in and brushed his lips against mine.

How could his lips be so soft? Softer than any lips I'd ever kissed. He leaned away but I grabbed hold of the back of his head and brought him back to me. No way was he running off this time.

The kiss wasn't so soft the second time, and he devoured my mouth with an intensity I had never felt in my life.

Both his arms came around me and he pulled me in close. Close into the same chest and stomach I'd just been drooling over. I slipped my hands under his shirt and let them slide across his stomach before allowing them to run up the silkiness of his back. He shuddered beneath my fingers. He bent over and lifted me off my feet, easily carrying me over to a stack of hay. Setting me down gently, he broke off the kiss. His eyes never left mine as he took off his shirt and laid it down behind me.

"Can I kiss you again?" he asked. I nodded.

Was he kidding? I'd wanted his mouth since the moment I saw him. He joined me on the hay, placing his hand behind my head and laying me back on his shirt. He lay almost on top of me, and my hands had their fill of his back. I could kiss him forever. His lips played with mine. Had he ever thought of doing this very same thing?

His lips had left me light-headed by the time he buried his face in my neck.

"You smell so good," he said. He planted tiny kisses along my jawline and I laughed.

"You do too," I told him.

One hand trailed along my arm while he nibbled on my jugular vein. He obviously wasn't inexperienced, either. I grinned. So much for being the total loner. I leaned my head back to give him better access to my throat.

He settled himself against me and his kisses on my neck grew more intense. He nuzzled up to under my ear and I almost moaned. I felt boneless, like a cat, and if I could have purred, I would've. Then he moved up to my ear and started nibbling my earlobe.

A bucket of cold water thrown over me couldn't have woken me up any quicker. I reacted without thinking.

"What are you doing?" I screeched, pushing him off me. I jumped up from the hay and wiped the back of my jeans off.

His eyes widened. "What do you mean? I was kissing you, we were kissing each other. What's wrong?"

My throat closed. How could I tell him without looking like some kind of freak? I *was* a freak. Different, weird, a freak. *How can I tell him that kissing my ears is like kissing my hearing aids?*

My eyes stung with tears and I turned away. The other guys I had made out with were so busy sticking their hands up my shirt, they never got around to nibbling my neck or kissing my ears.

I hid my humiliation in anger. "Next time I want to be kissed like that, I'll tell you!"

I tried to stomp out of the room, but he grabbed my arm. "What the hell are you talking about?"

I shook him off. "You thinking you could just kiss me or something." I tried to look furious, but a sob escaped. Stupid. I was so stupid. I wished I could take it all back.

To settle down into the hay again with his amazing lips on mine. How could I ever explain?

He watched the tears trailing down my cheeks and quirked an eyebrow in my direction. "You want to tell me what's going on?"

I swallowed. I owed him some kind of explanation. I mean, I'd practically jumped his bones and then freaked out on the poor guy. Wasn't his fault I had broken ears.

I crossed my arms and stared at a bag of dog food in the corner. "I don't like my ears touched. Ever." I kept my eyes firmly on the dog food. I didn't want to see the comprehension and pity in his eyes.

He reached out and took my hand. I snuck a look and saw his eyes filled with compassion. "All you had to do was tell me."

Everything—the sorority, Patrice telling me to stay away from Miller, my feelings about what had just happened—knotted up inside me.

His hands slid up my arms, gently tugging me toward him. He rubbed my back, the compassion and sympathy evident in the gentleness. Fury rose inside me. I didn't need gentleness. I didn't need sympathy. Not from anyone. Especially not from him.

"I shouldn't have to tell you. You should have *known*!"

His hands jerked back. "Why should I have known?" he bit out. "I don't even think of you as deaf half the time. You were sure acting like you were enjoying yourself, and I didn't even think about it."

"Maybe you should have." Unreasonable, I know, but I couldn't seem to help myself.

He drew in a deep breath as if to calm himself. "I thought we had something. I really like you a lot."

"How am I supposed to know that, the way you run off in school all the time, like you're embarrassed or something?" I stopped as the horrifying realization hit me in the chest like a boulder. "Oh, gawd, that's it! You're embarrassed by me—you don't want to be seen with the deaf girl! But I'm sure good enough to make out with, right?"

Anger lit his eyes with a terrifying darkness. I'd never seen anyone so livid. "If anyone is embarrassed to be seen with anyone, it's you, not me. The only time you want to be my friend is when your rich friends aren't around. I avoid you because I don't want to get in the way of you making friends—though why anyone would want to be friends with a crowd like that is beyond me! I know what they're like, and you wouldn't have a chance if they knew we were friends. So there!"

We stood looking at each other, breathing heavily as if we'd just run the mile in PE class.

"'So there'? How old are we? Ten?" Sarcasm dripped from my voice.

"Well, some of us are acting that way." Just as condescending.

"I'm not embarrassed to be friends with you," I said more quietly.

"Oh no? Who hid in the seat at Jerry's? And what was it Patrice said to you? Hanging around with me would give you the wrong reputation?"

The anger faded from his eyes and I spotted the hurt he couldn't quite hide under his bravado.

My stomach ached and my head hurt. I didn't want to lose him, but I really wanted to be in the sorority, too. Why did everything have to be so complicated? I made a sudden decision. "No, I'm not embarrassed and I'll prove it to you. I was invited to a party Friday night. Why don't you come with me as my date."

Oh my gawd. Did I just ask him out on a date? To a party? To *Patrice's* party? My heart pounded as I waited for his answer. Oh, gawd, what if he said no? He probably would, unsocial loner that he was. I squeezed my eyes shut. I didn't want to know. I'd ruined everything. Why couldn't I just keep my big-ass mouth shut? I felt a tap on my shoulder.

"I said okay."

"You said okay?"

"Yeah."

"Okay, then." I backed away from him until I hit the door. "I guess I'll be going home."

"Serena?"

"Yeah."

"Didn't you come to help with the dogs?"

I looked up to see his warm eyes laughing at me. *Jerk.* I giggled and wiped the tears out of my eyes. My body relaxed for the first time since I had seen him working with his shirt off. "Oh, yeah. What do you need me to do?"

I listened to his instructions, but inside my mind was going crazy. Gawd, I had a date! What the hell was Patrice going to do?

Eight

"Serena!"

I glanced over at a couple of girls walking toward me. I wasn't sure if they were the ones who had said my name. But one of them was smiling at me and I recognized her as one of the girls who had spoken to Patrice at the football game.

She held out her hand. "My name is Meredith; this is Annie. Do you have a minute?"

Meredith's dark eyes appraised me coolly as she shoved a strand of her auburn hair behind her ear. Annie was shorter but carried herself with authority. They didn't even seem like high school girls, they were so confident and smooth. All in all, pretty damn intimidating.

I nodded, unable to speak. Just being in their presence made me feel too fat, too dark, and too frumpy, even in the new pastel-colored clothes Mom had bought me.

"I know Patrice has filled you in on our sorority, and I wanted to let you know you've been approved."

Meredith flashed me a game-show-girl smile, as though I had just won the Showcase Showdown or something. I tried to look properly excited without being overeager.

"Of course, you still have to make it through initiation week," added Annie.

Okay, serious mode. I nodded and furrowed my brow. "Of course."

Meredith frowned. "But I'm sure you'll make it through just fine." She looked around the empty hall and I started to get antsy. The late bell for last period should be ringing in a few minutes.

Annie must have been thinking the same thing, 'cause she jumped in. "The other reason we wanted to talk to you is we wanted to ask you a favor."

Why was I not surprised?

Meredith nodded. "Annie and I are in charge of choosing next year's sorority president." She gave an adorable grin that wrinkled her nose. "Well, basically Annie and I are in charge of everything! So far our top picks are in a dead heat. We're really having a hard time making up our minds."

Annie nodded. "We have Patrice, the bitch, or Sonya, the slut."

Meredith shot her a dirty look. "Not in front of an initiate," she snapped.

Annie looked as though she was going to say something,

but bit her lip. Meredith turned back to me as if nothing had happened.

"That's where you come in," she said. "We want you to spy on them. Use your special talents to see if you can dig up any dirt on them."

"Dirt?" I asked stupidly. Another spy job. Who wasn't I spying on these days?

"Yeah. Find out what they are planning, how loyal they are—stuff like that. Oh, and especially who they're sleeping with."

"Sleeping with?"

Annie and Meredith exchanged glances, a look that said, *"Are we really letting this moron in?"*

Okay, I knew I sounded stupid, but come on!

I pulled it together. "Oh, right. Gotcha. Not a problem."

The bell sounded and I backed up. "Dirt. Totally." I ran backward into a girl rushing into home ec. "Oops, sorry!" I whirled around and jogged off, before my face started glowing like a nuclear meltdown.

Okay. So I was spying on Sonya for Patrice, on Patrice and Sonya for the two senior beauty queens, and on everyone else for my friends. I was gonna have to write this stuff down.

I was in such a hurry, I almost ran into Craig the blockhead on my way into the office. I moved around him and slipped behind the desk.

He glowered at me. "I have an appointment with Mrs. Chandler."

I looked around but couldn't see Mrs. Watson, who usually handled the appointments.

"Mrs. Watson's not here," I said. I was always good at stating the obvious.

"Duh. Just check me in and tell Mrs. Chandler I'm here."

I handed him the sign-in sheet and went back to tell Mrs. Chandler that her two o'clock appointment was in. I would have used the phone to tell her but hadn't been trained on it so I didn't dare. Besides, I didn't know how loud the speaker was. I needed it really loud—my cell was turned up to maximum volume so I could hear with my hearing aids and so was our home phone. Plus, with my luck I'd probably get the school intercom system or something.

I came back and gestured for him to enter. He made hand motions as though he were doing sign language and I itched to slap him.

I looked at the stack of papers to file and sighed. Might as well get started. And yet . . . why was Craig with the guidance counselor? I looked around. No one in the office paid any attention to me, and Mrs. Watson hadn't appeared. I grabbed a sheaf of papers and snuck back toward the offices. When I reached the huge in-box cabinet, I pretended to put papers into teacher's slots.

Perfect view of the guidance counselor's office window. I couldn't see Craig's face—just the back of his head—but I had a perfect view of Mrs. Chandler's mouth.

"I tried to tell you last year, Craig. You're not graduating this year. That's why I recommended summer school."

Craig must have answered, because Mrs. Chandler's lips thinned into a flat, angry line.

"Summer school isn't for losers—it's for people who haven't got enough credits to graduate. I don't even know if summer school is going to be enough now. You may have to come to school again next year for a term."

Mrs. Chandler stopped speaking for a minute. I saw her take a deep breath. "If the talent scouts come to talk to me about a possible football scholarship for you, I'm going to have to tell them what I am telling you now. You're not graduating this year."

Holy crap! I took my papers and scampered back to the office. Now, this should make Patrice happy!

The dean of students walked by. "Mr. Lutz?" Would I ever be able to say that name without smiling? "Have you seen Mrs. Watson?"

"She's out sick today. Just go ahead and do what you normally do."

I smiled at him. "Okay."

After he had gone, I opened the drawer containing the signed hall passes Mrs. Watson always kept on hand so she didn't have to write them out all the time. My heart pounded as I reached in and grabbed a handful. I looked at the stack in my hand and put back a few. No sense in going overboard. I swallowed and slipped the hall passes into the pocket of my jeans. I looked around. No one was watching me, so I grabbed a pink message notepad.

Trying to look official, I scribbled a couple of messages, one for Patrice and one for Rachel.

Part of me couldn't believe that I was doing this just to make my friends happy. The other part was kind of having fun.

Rachel's seventh-period class was English lit, while Patrice had drama. I walked to the door with a stern frown on my face as if I had serious business to attend to, even though my hands were shaking. This had to work.

No one stopped me. The halls were quiet except when I passed classes with open doors. I found the room Rachel was in and, heart pounding, knocked on the door. The teacher opened it. "Yes?"

"I have a message for Rachel Conner." The teacher looked at the student staff ID hanging around my neck and then at the note I held out.

"Rachel, you're wanted in the office immediately."

Rachel came out frowning until she saw me. Her mouth made an O of surprise.

"Come on, let's go get Patrice," I said after the door had shut.

We hurried down the hall, and I repeated the performance. It was harder this time because Rachel was hiding out of sight from the teacher, trying not to laugh, which almost made me laugh.

Patrice walked out with a carefully composed blank face. As soon as she figured out what I'd done, though, she went nuts.

"Oh my God, we've corrupted you!" she told me out of earshot of the teacher. "I knew getting you into the office was a kick-ass idea."

Rachel grabbed my arm. "Now what?"

"I've got news that couldn't wait. Come on."

I led them into the nearest girls' bathroom.

"Okay, what's so important you had to drag me out of drama—thank you, by the way—to tell us?" Patrice asked.

Rachel applied lip gloss in the mirror and smacked her lips. "Aren't you going to get in trouble?"

"Nah, Mrs. Watson's gone. I don't think anyone will even notice I've left."

I felt almost light-headed as I prepared myself. I knew what was at risk here. It could all blow up in my face. I could end up on the outside again. But how much could I really compromise myself? I looked in the mirror and hardly recognized the person staring back at me. No eyebrow ring, no hoodie, no black. I wasn't going to do without Miller, too.

I turned to the girls I hoped were really my friends. Patrice was my target. Rachel was there as support in case it went badly.

"First off, before I tell you the two amazing pieces of gossip I have for you, I have a question for Patrice."

Patrice wrinkled her forehead. "For me? What?"

I cleared my throat. "I want to bring Miller to your party as my date." There. It was out. I held out my hand at the cold look on Patrice's face. "Before you say no, I have something that will sweeten the deal." I took a deep breath and pulled the passes out of my pocket. "Signed hall passes."

Patrice's mouth hung open. She looked over at Rachel, who had the same look of shock on her face. "I repeat, we were *so* right to set this chick up in the office." She turned back to me and shrugged. "Okay, whatever. Even though I still don't know why you'd want to go out with him, bring him along to the party—I don't care." Patrice's mouth twisted in begrudging respect. "You are one ballsy chick."

It worked! I let out the breath I'd been holding. "Now for the good stuff. Guess what football player has college scouts after him but can't go to college because he's *not* graduating?"

Patrice clutched her chest. "Oh my God, it's not Scott, is it? Say it's not Scott!"

"It's not Scott."

"Oh, thank God. Unless you just said that because I told you to." Patrice's eyes narrowed.

"No, idiot. It's Craig!"

Rachel clapped her hand over her mouth. "Get out!"

"No way!" Patrice breathed. "His father is going to slaughter him. As in murder."

Rachel nodded. "Yeah, he's been driving Craig to get a football scholarship for years."

"No wonder he's such a gem," I muttered.

We heard someone coming in to use the bathroom, so we sprang into action, washing our hands and acting as though we were supposed to be there. When we saw it was just a student, we relaxed and waited until she left.

"I can't believe this. I wonder if Scott knows."

I shrugged. "I dunno. I didn't see him leave. I didn't want to get busted."

The bell rang and other students filed in. It was safe for us to be in the halls, so we left.

"So, are you going to tell Scott?" Rachel asked.

Patrice didn't answer until we had reached our lockers, "I don't know. Should I?"

I bit my thumb. "He'll want to know where you found out."

Rachel nodded and slung her arm around me. "Yeah, we don't want to jeopardize our source here."

Patrice stopped in the middle of her locker combination, her gaze moving past Rachel and me. She said something, but I didn't hear it.

"What?"

Patrice jerked her head toward the end of our row of lockers. "Look. So how come Kelly's boyfriend is hanging all over her sister?"

I looked to where she had gestured and saw Kelly's boyfriend, Tyler, and Kayla talking quietly. They weren't exactly hanging all over each other, but it definitely looked intense.

Patrice leaned forward. "See what you can find out."

I focused on their mouths.

"I can't go out with you—Kelly would kill me," Kayla was saying.

Tyler grinned at her. "You weren't thinking about her last night when you were kissing me under the bleachers. It was just us then."

Kayla pouted but moved out of my vision, so I missed what she said.

Tyler continued, "Nah, it was all about you. Your sister can't kiss as good as you can."

I choked and coughed, and Tyler looked up. Patrice and Rachel busied themselves at their lockers as I pretended to be interested in the architecture of the commons area.

Kayla came up to us moments later. "Hi, guys. Tyler was asking how I did on the history pop quiz." She tossed back her highlights and smiled at me. "Awesome, thanks to our girl here."

Rachel stuck some books in her locker. "Yeah, she saved my butt."

"Are you going to Jerry's?" Kayla asked.

"Mmm. I think so," Patrice said.

"Okay, I might see you there. I have to go find Kel. Later." She sauntered down the hall and we all remained quiet until she turned the corner.

Patrice tossed her hair in an imitation of Kayla. "So, was Tyler's interest in Kayla purely academic?"

I snorted. "He asked her something all right, but not about a pop quiz. He asked her out."

"NO!" Rachel said, her eyes wide.

"Today just keeps getting better and better," Patrice said, smirking. "Serena, you just may be the best thing that ever happened to this school."

I waved my hand in front of me in a royal gesture. "Why, thank you, but . . . there's more."

"More?" Rachel's voice squeaked on the end, causing one of my aids to squeal. "How could there be more?"

"They made out last night under the bleachers."

Patrice shook her head, laughing. "This couldn't get any better."

Rachel flicked her locker shut. "Unless you're Kelly. It's not gonna be awesome for her when she finds out."

Patrice sobered. "Yeah, that's true. Who wants to break it to her?"

"I ain't telling her," Rachel said.

I raised my hands in front of me. "Don't look at me. I'm just the revealer. It's not up to me to do anything about what I learn."

"Chickens," Patrice said. "But we all agree someone should tell her, right?"

Rachel and I nodded.

"Somebody's got to. I mean, if it were your sister,

wouldn't you want to know?" Rachel asked.

"My parents had my big brother and me. Then they had the wisdom to stop," Patrice said.

"I'm an only child. I think my parents decided to stop while they *weren't* ahead so they wouldn't have another deaf baby."

Patrice and Rachel both looked at me. I felt heat rising in my cheeks. Where had that freaking come from? "What? I'm fine." I forced my voice to be calm and steady. "Really," I stressed.

For once Patrice didn't push it. "Okay, so I'm the chosen executioner, but no way am I going in alone."

"Fair enough,." I agreed.

Jerry's was busy when we got there, but we managed to grab a table and looked around for Kelly. She and Tyler were sitting in the back holding hands.

Patrice moaned. "How come I feel like the Grinch Who Stole Christmas?"

"Come on, Grinch, let's get it over with," Rachel said, waving Kelly to our table.

Kelly hurried over, looking like a cross between Jessica Simpson and Paris Hilton. "What's up, girlfriends?" She scooted in next to Rachel. "Hurry up. Tyler's awaiting."

Silence descended on the table. Kelly looked from Patrice to Rachel and her face fell. "What? What's happened?"

Behind Patrice's head I could see Kayla sidling up to Tyler's table. Uh-oh.

Patrice chewed on her top lip for a moment. "I hate to have to be the one to tell you this, but Kayla and Tyler are having some kind of thing."

Nothing subtle about Patrice.

A look of wide-eyed disbelief swept over Kelly's face. "Nuh-uh."

"We overheard them today," Patrice continued, "and they were talking about making out under the bleachers last night."

Kelly shook her head. "No. Tyler was at practice until late last night. He told me."

"Scott called me at five-thirty and said practice got out early. Where was Kayla?" Patrice asked.

Kelly went silent. The truth struggled on her face. "She was studying at the library."

Patrice raised an eyebrow. "Kayla? At the library?"

"So how did you overhear them, anyway?"

Patrice's eyes slid over to me and Kelly caught the glance. "Oh my God, you read their lips," she said, looking at me.

I crouched down in my seat.

Rachel put her hand on Kelly's arm and pointed over to where Tyler sat with Kayla. They were far enough apart, but from where we sat, we saw Tyler touch Kayla's leg under the table. She playfully slapped it away.

"Be-yotch!" Kelly hurtled out of the booth and toward her sister with the speed of lightning. Kayla saw her coming and huddled down, protecting her head with her arms. Kelly did a swan dive onto the table, knocking glasses and silverware every which way. She grabbed handfuls of Kayla's hair and began yanking the expensive salon highlights out by the roots. Kayla's screech could probably have been heard all the way to my old school.

Tyler moved back toward the wall but couldn't leave because the table had him trapped.

"You sleaze! You ho!"

Kayla started fighting back in earnest, but Satan himself would have been no match for Kelly's fury.

"Catfight!" somebody screamed, and the rest of the patrons rushed in for a better view, except for an elderly couple who'd probably wandered in by mistake.

I covered my ears to keep my aids from squealing. "I move that we go!" I yelled.

Rachel turned toward me. "I second the motion."

I couldn't see what Patrice said, but she hopped out of the booth, so I figured it was unanimous.

We slipped outside and ran, laughing for Patrice's car.

Rachel slammed the door shut and locked it. "Oh my God, that was so funny!"

Patrice started the car, still laughing. "I never knew Kelly was so fast. She should do track!"

"Or girls' football. Did you see that tackle?" I added.

"Poor Kelly, though," Rachel said.

"Yeah." Patrice started laughing again. "Sorry, it was just so funny!"

We rode the rest of the way home in near silence except for the occasional giggle.

But did I do the right thing? I wondered, after Patrice had dropped me off.

I mean, it had seemed like a good idea at the time, but guilt pinged in my chest as I thought about swiping the hall passes. Hey, it had worked. I got Patrice to say Miller could come to the party. I shrugged. And Kelly did need to know. I'd deal with my conscience later.

Right now I had bigger things on my mind. Like how to get Mom and Dad to agree to let me go to the party.

I decided on the relaxed approach, as though it had never entered my mind that they wouldn't let me go. Dinner was the perfect time.

"Patrice is throwing a party after the homecoming game on Friday," I opened, when we were almost done with our meal. "It's going to be casual because the guys will be showering and coming right from the game."

"I thought the dance was after the game," Dad said, looking at me over his glasses.

I took a sip of my milk and shook my head. "Nah. I thought so too, but they changed that several years ago."

I eyed Mom, who kept eating without commenting.

"I think Miller is going to take me right after the game. Rachel was going to take me until Miller decided to go."

Mom put down her fork and Dad looked from me to

Mom. Obviously he'd be abstaining from this one. Like Switzerland. I turned to Mom and continued.

"I think Patrice is going to have tons of food there, so we'll probably go straight from the game to the party."

I speared my last green bean with my fork and put it into my mouth, even though it tasted like sand.

"I don't know if this is such a good idea," Mom said.

"If what's a good idea?" Good girl. Perfect amount of surprise.

"Going to a party with a guy."

Mother hover alert.

Ha! If she only knew half the things I had done at my old school. *Okay, stay relaxed.* I forced my lips into a gentle, amused smile. "Mom, it's not just any guy—it's Miller. He's practically my cousin."

Mom shook her head. "Just how much do we know about this kid?"

So he went from "a guy" to "this kid."

And the helicopter started its engines.

Stay in control. "He's going to be a vet and he's a 4.0 student. Plus, he's just a friend. We're only going to a party together."

Mom frowned and picked up her fork. "I'm not sure I like the idea of you going to a party with a bunch of kids you hardly know."

And the blades started whirling.

Stay reasonable. "Mom, you've met Patrice and Rachel

a couple of times and you like them. Plus, didn't you move here so I could be a part of the community?"

There. I knew I could throw that in somewhere.

"Are there going to be adults there?" Mom asked.

Stay calm. "Patrice's folks gave her permission to have the party." I gave a light laugh. "It's not like one of those bashes you hear about with alcohol and stuff."

Mom frowned, causing her forehead to bunch up in worried wrinkles. "A lot of parties get way out of hand."

Okay, so maybe it had been a tactical error to mention alcohol.

Stay focused. I shook my head. "This won't be like that."

"But you didn't mention if her parents were actually going to be there," Dad reminded me.

I shot him a glance. His eyes were wide and innocent, but I could detect the sparkle. So much for Switzerland.

"I think they're going somewhere for a while, but will be home before the party is over," I admitted.

"I don't like that at all. If you think I'm going to just let you run off to a party with no supervision, you have another think coming."

And we had liftoff. Mother hover in full force.

Dad took a sip of his wine. "I hardly think that she's running off anywhere. Miller's a nice, responsible guy and the party is at a friend's house. No, there isn't supervision for the entire time, but I think if all the kids know her parents are coming home, they will behave reasonably well."

So Dad wasn't on Mom's side after all! In fact, he had just picked up an antiaircraft gun and shot down the mother hover. I suppressed the urge to cheer.

Mom wavered. "I don't know."

"Please, Mom." Full-on-boo-boo face. I'd been holding back until the very right moment.

"Okay. If your dad thinks it's okay, I won't argue."

Score!

I jumped up and kissed Mom and then Dad. "You guys are the greatest!"

I forced myself to walk sedately from the room when I wanted to dance and shout. I'd won! I had a date and was going to a party!

Once upstairs I threw myself across my bed in triumph. I'd done it!

My phone vibrated in my pocket, and I pulled it out and flipped it open.

It was a text from Patrice.

Hey. U said U had two pieces of gossip and U only told us 1. What was the other 1?

I took a deep breath. I didn't know if aligning myself with Patrice in this whole sorority mess was the right thing to do, but I couldn't be on Sonya's side, that was for damn sure.

So I texted back.

I got a little visit from Meredith and Annie 2day. Will talk 2 U 2morrow b4 school.

There was a long pause and I wondered what she would say.

Can't 2morrow morning. Sorority business. Will talk later.

That was it.

I lay back down on the bed, most of my earlier exultation gone. Who knew that having friends would be so effing complicated?

Nine

Patrice came up to me before first period the next day. "You look fabulous!"

She eyed me up and down as I dragged myself in a slow circle. Mom kept buying me new stuff. It pissed me off how much she enjoyed my new look. Where was the fun in that? My customary hoodie had been replaced with a tiny short-waisted jacket. I wasn't sure I liked the way the stretchy material hugged my chest. I felt so exposed. But I also felt more girly. Not a bad way to feel, I'd decided. Though I wouldn't be telling Mom that anytime soon.

"You likey?" I asked.

Patrice nodded. "Very hot. I have to run, but I didn't want you to think I had forgotten our conversation. I'm just really busy gearing up for initiation week. Oh, and don't make plans for lunch today. It's interview time!"

She winked and flashed me a conspirator's smile before rushing off.

What interview? I had to interview? My stomach dropped. Freaking great.

By third period I was so tense about the interview, I forgot to be weirded out about seeing Miller. He no longer acted like I was the plagued chick in school, but he was still a bit cool, as if we hadn't swapped spit and felt each other up.

I sat at my desk and pulled out my books. Funny how different it was to make out with someone you really cared about compared to someone you just liked.

Rachel tapped me on the shoulder and I turned. "You nervous about the interviews?"

"Yeah—what's that about, anyway?"

"That means they've made up the list and are just interviewing you to make sure you're sorority material. It's mostly just a formality. But last year Darcy Freeman blew the interview and wasn't invited. She used to be a total prep. Now she gets into fights and skips school and all sorts of stuff. It's because she didn't get in." Rachel nodded, her blue eyes solemn.

Gawd, that would suck. "How did she blow the interview?" I didn't want to make the same mistake.

Rachel shrugged. "I dunno. But I do know that the only friends she has are outcasts."

Ms. Fisher called the class to order and I turned back to my history book. But my mind reeled. One mistake and

Darcy Freeman was branded a loser for the rest of her school life. I gulped. I'd seen Darcy Freeman. She was cute and preppy. What chance did I have?

Miller dashed through the door and apologized for being late. He flashed me a smile before hitting the books. I hoped no one would make a big deal about us going to the party together. Now that I was so close to being in, I really didn't want to blow it.

I glanced over at Miller, whose dark hair had flopped into his eyes as he studied. Just thinking about those electrifying kisses made me quiver.

By the time the bell rang, I thought I'd read the same paragraph twelve times without making any sense of it. I sighed.

Rachel tapped me on the shoulder. "Showtime."

Like she needed to remind me.

We headed out into the hall. Miller had disappeared, but I had more pressing things on my mind. Like that bloody freaking interview. "I think Sonya's going to blackball me," I said.

Rachel's forehead wrinkled. "Why would you think that?"

I shrugged. "'Cause I've seen her and Patrice arguing over it. She thinks I'm a freak."

"Well, I'm sure she didn't mean . . ." Rachel started to say, but I gave her a look and she shut up.

"She's just really driven to be first in everything," she said a minute later, apologetically. "You know her mom's on the PTA, right?" At my nod she continued. "Sonya's big sister was always first in everything and she was the favorite. I guess Sonya probably felt like an afterthought."

I stared at Rachel, then shrugged. Like I was supposed to feel sorry for her?

The cafeteria was packed and Rachel stopped at our table. "I can't eat," she said, her complexion even paler than usual.

Kelly looked up. "I don't want to hear a word about you being nervous. How would you like to go to the interview looking like this?"

She leaned forward and stuck her lip out. Like she needed to—it was already swollen and cut in two places.

"Your sister looks worse than you do," Rachel remarked.

"Good. The ho." Kelly went back to staring glumly at her yogurt.

"Want me to get us some water?" I asked.

Rachel nodded and I turned toward the vending machines. I spotted Sonya talking to Kayla across the room. Kayla did look like crap. One eye glowed black and blue from across the cafeteria and her jaw looked swollen. Forget Patrice—Kelly was the one to be scared of around here. Chick could kick ass. I focused on Sonya's mouth.

"Patrice isn't going to know what hit her," Sonya said. "I'm not only going to swipe her man, but the presidency, too."

I couldn't see what Kayla said, but it made Sonya laugh.

"Easy. I've already slept with Scott. And all I have to do is prove that I would be a better president than Patrice. Which won't be hard. As junior class secretary, I have access to certain things."

Suddenly her eyes, which had been scanning the crowd, zeroed in on me. I froze. Our eyes locked and for a moment I couldn't move. Then I waved a hand at her and smiled. I turned away and shoved coins into the machine, my heart racing. This was the kind of stuff Patrice was looking for. Of course, I had no proof and I didn't even know what Sonya was planning. But I knew she was planning something.

"Hi! Thirsty?"

I turned and Sonya was next to me, smiling widely. The first friendly smile she'd ever given me. "I'm getting one for Rachel, too," I told her.

"Oh, cool." She leaned against the machine as I punched in the numbers. "You know, I've been thinking . . ."

Don't hurt yourself.

". . . and I think that you would be a great asset to the sorority after all."

She sounded like a cheerleader, like she'd just presented me with a gift beyond measure. I wanted to smack her.

I turned and knit my brows. "Really? And why do you think that?"

She shrugged. "Your gift could come in really handy. As long as it's used for good and not evil." Her laugh came out forced. "Plus, you've really changed your look lately. Everybody's noticed. Nice."

Wow. She must have been really worried that I was going to sell her out. Scaredy Sonya.

Meredith walked up and tapped her on the shoulder. "It's time," she said.

Sonya nodded and waved at me. "See you in a few!"

I walked back to Rachel and Kelly. Kayla had come over to our table. She sat at the opposite end from her sister. Waiting for the call like the rest of us, no doubt. I saw Patrice, Sonya, Annie, and Meredith heading into the girls' restroom on the other side of the cafeteria.

Kelly cracked her knuckles nervously while Kayla just looked smug—or as smug as she could, given that her eye looked like chopped meat.

Rachel's skin had taken on a green color, and she leaned her head onto her hands. "I think I'm going to throw up."

I patted her back and handed her some water. "You'll be fine. Don't let them get to you. They're just chicks like we are." Like I should talk. It felt like somebody was playing hoops in my stomach.

Just then Darcy Freeman walked up to our table. Her short white-blond hair was tucked behind ears that had, miracle of miracles in this school, several piercings each. She put her hands onto the table and leaned forward. "Hey, chickies. Ready for the big scary interview?"

Kayla and Kelly looked stunned. Rachel gave her a polite smile.

"What interview?"

Darcy laughed. "Oh please, I've been here before. I just have one word of advice: Run. Run for the hills. Do you honestly think anyone is going to give a rat's ass if Thing One and Thing Two like you? Do you really want to give them the power to humiliate you for a week so you can be an It girl?"

"You're just bitter 'cause you didn't get in," Kayla shot back.

"Is that what you think, Barbie?" Darcy laughed again. "Nah, I just feel it's my patriotic duty to warn all you newbies. Run, before you become a carbon copy of everyone else."

How come I felt like she was directing every word toward me? Even after she walked off, leaving the rest of us silent, my heart skittered in my chest and her words echoed in my head over and over. *Carbon copy of everyone else. Carbon copy of everyone else.* I looked down at my tiny pink T-shirt and jacket.

She had a point.

Annie walked up to our table. "Kayla? Can we talk to you?"

Kayla smirked at the rest of us and followed Annie to the bathroom.

I glanced over at Kelly. "Are you sure you guys are twins?"

"Sometimes I wonder." She frowned and then put her fingers to her lip and moaned.

Rachel wrinkled her forehead. "So what are you going to do about Tyler?"

Kelly sighed, her eyes filled with pain. "Ditch him. I could never kiss him again without thinking of him kissing my sister." She shuddered.

"That would be almost as bad as finding out your boyfriend had kissed your mom," Rachel said.

We stared at her. "I'm just saying!" she protested.

Kelly shrugged. "It just sucks 'cause we've been going out since sixth grade. I thought it was long term, you know?"

Rachel nodded toward the bathroom and we turned to look. Kayla and Sonya came out and hugged before Kayla came skipping back to us.

"Your turn," she told me. "Good luck."

The tone of her voice indicated I was going to need it.

I'd had enough. I was already nervous; I didn't need her crap, too. "If you want, I can help you out. I can smack your other eye so you match."

Silence. Then Kelly giggled. I turned and walked over to where the keepers of the sorority waited.

I was so not in the mood for this.

Meredith and Annie were sitting on cafeteria chairs when I entered. They smiled at me. Patrice winked and Sonya checked something off in her notebook.

Meredith indicated the floor. "Have a seat."

The bathroom floor? Gross! But I sat anyway, my heart in my throat.

Annie said something, but I was so nervous, I couldn't quite catch it.

"What?"

Sonya exchanged an "I told you so" look with Annie.

"What?" I asked again, feeling like an idiot.

Meredith flipped her hair over her shoulder. "We just wanted to make sure you know that everything we talk about remains confidential."

"Of course." I leaned back on my arms and tried to look calm and confident. Might have worked, except the sweat beading on my forehead was a dead giveaway.

"Why do you want to be in the sorority?" Annie asked.

My mind went blank. Why *did* I want to be in the sorority? What were my reasons? I had reasons, didn't I? As the silence lengthened, Patrice leaned forward, her face tense.

I had to say something. "Because I want the social opportunities the sorority offers?"

I wished I sounded more confident, but they nodded encouragingly.

"And I really want to fit in here."

Oh my gawd. Did I say that?

A moment of naked silence spun out between us before Meredith nodded. "Do you have any questions?" she asked.

I shook my head. I thought I'd said enough.

Annie referred to the clipboard in her hand. "Okay, then

we'll tell you a little bit about the procedure and the soror-ity. It was founded in the 1970s to discuss how the women's movement would affect the lives of female students. Since then it's become more exclusive, until—"

"Does the sorority still do that?" I asked, surprising myself and everyone else.

Annie peered at the clipboard as if that would give her the answer.

Patrice wrinkled her brow in confusion. "Do what?"

I shifted on the floor. Would I ever be able to keep my big mouth shut? "Meet to talk about women's rights and stuff."

More silence.

Meredith forced a smile. "Personally, I have all the rights I can handle."

"It's more of a social thing," Annie added.

"Great!" I enthused, feeling like a moron.

Sonya darted a quick glance at the others. "We should hurry—we have a lot of girls to get through."

"How many are trying to join?" Gawd, why couldn't I just shut up?

"Twelve this year," Patrice answered. "We're trying to get more exclusive."

Annie leaned forward. "About the initiation—there are five days and one task for each day. They take place out-side of school 'cause the administration can't get any wind of this. We'll give you the task the night before by e-mail or text message. On Friday, if you make it, we'll have the initiation ceremony and you'll get more information about the sorority itself."

Patrice grinned. "That's about it. Do you have any questions?"

I shook my head. I'd asked enough already.

"Good. Why don't you send Rachel over?" Meredith instructed.

I was dismissed. I noticed Sonya didn't jump up to hug *me*. I pointed to Rachel when I got back to the table, and she took a deep breath before heading over. Kayla had disappeared, leaving a depressed Kelly alone.

"You'll be fine," I reassured her. "We'll all be fine."

At least, I hoped so. But I couldn't get Darcy's comments out of my mind. I wasn't a carbon copy, was I?

I was still feeling down by the time I got into the office later that afternoon. Mrs. Watson had come back sniffly and anxious to make up for time she could have spent pampering her student staff. The plate of cookies she'd brought were on the counter and I had the misfortune to actually eat one. The flavor would have made Betty Crocker turn over in her grave.

"HAVE ANOTHER COOKIE," Mrs. Watson urged.

I declined. "I'm still so stuffed from lunch."

"I'LL WRAP SOME UP FOR YOU TO TAKE HOME TO YOUR FAMILY. I DON'T WANT TO TAKE THEM HOME. I HAVE TO WATCH MY WAISTLINE, YOU

KNOW." She gave me a scrunched-up smile and patted my arm.

I went back to filing. I'd been afraid that Mrs. Watson would notice the missing hall passes, but she hadn't mentioned it.

Suddenly the peace and quiet of the office shattered when the door crashed open and Tyler and Miller were hauled into the office by a teacher I didn't know.

"Sit down," he commanded. "And don't even look at each other."

Tyler rolled his eyes, one of which was turning the brightest shade of purple I'd ever seen. If he and Kayla were together, they'd be a matched set. He took a seat in one of the waiting chairs, but Miller stayed standing.

"I said sit down." The teacher gave Miller a little shove.

Miller sat and crossed his arms in front of him. He had blood coming from his nose and Mrs. Watson hurried to get him a tissue.

I froze. I wanted to go to Miller, but the black warning of his eyes stopped me.

"Go get Mr. Lutz!" the teacher barked.

I hurried down the hall. What the hell had happened? I knocked on the door. "Mr. Lutz, I think you should come quick."

Neither boy had moved when I returned. My stomach sank. The grim faces said something was radically wrong.

The teacher glared at them before turning to Mr. Lutz, who came in right behind me. "These two decided to have a knock-down drag-out in my classroom and I wasn't sure what you wanted me to do with them."

Oh my gawd. I couldn't even pretend to go back to work.

Mr. Lutz gave Miller a dark look. "Just can't stay out of trouble, can you?"

Miller stayed silent and Mr. Lutz heaved an exaggerated sigh. "All right, go see Mrs. Chandler. Tyler, I'll talk to you in my office."

I stood in shock as everyone left the main office. I'd talked to Miller after lunch and everything had been *fine*. What could have happened?

I went back to filing but looked for an opportunity to sneak down the hall to see what was going on. Unfortunately, Mrs. Watson decided to stay at the helm and I didn't get the chance.

Mr. Lutz came out of his office, said something to Mrs. Watson, and then walked back to Mrs. Chandler's office.

"SERENA COULD YOU HAND ME A WARNING SHEET OUT OF THE DISCIPLINARY-ACTIONS FILE?"

Only one? I found the correct file and handed the yellow slip to Mrs. White.

I filed and watched. A few minutes later Mr. Lutz strode down the hallway.

He said something to Mrs. Watson who turned back to me.

"SERENA, COULD YOU HAND ME THE TEMPORARY-SUSPENSION SHEET FROM THE SAME FILE?"

Suspension? I handed Mrs. Watson the sheet.

"I just hate when one of our students gets suspended," Mrs. Watson told Mr. Lutz.

I see she doesn't yell at *him*, I thought, getting into a position so I could read Mr. Lutz's lips. He was speaking too quietly for me to hear.

Mr. Lutz shook his head. "Neither boy will tell me what happened so we are going to have to take Ronald's word for it. Tyler was just sitting there and Miller attacked him."

"Oh, there has to be more than that," Mrs. Watson said. "He's been doing so much better this year."

Mr. Lutz shrugged. "Once a troublemaker, always a troublemaker."

Mrs. Watson tsk-tsked as Mr. Lutz went back into his office with a filled-out warning sheet.

My throat tightened with tears. No way would Miller just attack someone. Why hadn't he defended himself? There had to be a reason. And I already knew Tyler was a snake.

Tyler came out of Mr. Lutz's office. He spotted me standing by the filing cabinet and glared at me, his eyes shooting sparks.

Bitch, he mouthed, without making a noise.

I heard him loud and clear.

My stomach seized with panic and my skin crawled. I

had a sudden premonition that whatever the fight was about, I was in the middle of it.

Miller stalked down the hall with his jaw tight and the red suspension slip in his hand. He shoved the door open with one hand and left without even glancing at me.

I hesitated for a few moments, then went after him. No way was he leaving without talking to me.

I dashed out the door and down the hall toward the doors leading out to the parking lot.

"Miller!" I yelled, seeing him at the bottom of the stairs. He either didn't hear or wasn't stopping, and I hurtled down the stairs after him. He exited the building and I followed.

"Miller, wait!" I grabbed the shoulder of his jacket and yanked. "Would you wait?"

He turned, and at the look in his eyes, my hand dropped off his arm.

"I don't want to talk about this," he said tightly.

"You have to; you can't just run off and—"

"I'm not running off, Serena—I was asked to leave. No, I was *ordered* to leave." He held up the red paper in his hand. "I'm not allowed on school property for three days."

I ignored that. "Tell me what happened."

"No. It wouldn't do any good."

His eyes evaded mine and I was surer than ever that the fight had something to do with me.

"You have to tell me, especially if I'm involved."

He looked at me directly. "Why would you think that?"

"Because Tyler called me a bitch on his way out the door. I figured it had something to do with yesterday." I looked up at him, pleading. "Now, will you just tell me?"

His shoulders slumped. He must have really wanted to keep it from me.

"He mentioned what happened yesterday and said something about making sure you never read lips again, and then he called you a name."

My stomach heaved at the threat, but I pretended it didn't matter. "Miller, I've been called worse. Names don't hurt. Okay, they hurt a little," I amended when I saw his sharp look. "But not from someone like Tyler. He's scum. You don't need to fight my battles. I've been fighting them all my life."

"I just don't want you to have to fight them alone anymore." He cleared his throat and looked away.

I took a deep, shuddering breath. "I know, but you can't get yourself kicked out of school to fight them."

"God, what am I going to do?" He walked over to his truck and leaned against the door. "I hate telling Alan and Shirley I got kicked out."

I gave him a little shove. "Hey, I'm their niece, remember? They're going to thank you for beating the guy up."

Miller gave me a weak smile and glanced at his watch just as the school bell rang. "I've got to jet. I have to get to work."

"Go. I'll talk to you later, and don't forget to take care

of your nose before you get to the vet clinic." I stepped back from the truck and watched him leave. He had fought for me. No one had ever fought for me, except my parents and teachers. Whatever it was we had, it was real. I tried to sort out my feelings. Bummed, because I now had more enemies at this school than I had ever had. In fact, I had more enemies than people who had known my name in the old school. But I also had someone who cared enough to kick some ass when those enemies dissed me. In spite of all the turmoil flickering through my mind, that pleased me.

I trudged back into the school, hoping I wouldn't run into anyone. I didn't want to fill anyone in on today's gossip. I just wanted to go home.

No such luck. Sonya cornered me at my locker.

"Okay, spill it. Everyone knows about the fight. Did you find out what happened?"

"I don't know what you're talking about, and if I did, I wouldn't tell you anyway."

"Ooohh. Feeling a little hormonal?" Gone was all the simpering sweetness from earlier.

I shoved my books into my backpack. As much as I didn't want to deal with her, something told me that pissing her off right now wouldn't be a good idea. After all, she and Patrice were in charge of my humiliation next week, not to mention the rest of my school social life. "I'm sorry. I don't feel good and I really have to go."

I turned away, but Sonya clamped a hand on my shoulder. "Glad that's it, because I'd hate to think you were trying to mess with me."

I shook her arm off and started for home. Too bad it wasn't as easy to shake off the icy glare she gave me as I left.

Ten

"You better hurry up and change," Mom said as soon as I walked into the kitchen after school. "I have to drop you off at the kennels. You told Shirley and Alan you would help out when Miller worked. One of them will bring you home when you're done."

"I know, I know!" Mom's confidence in my time-management ability was staggering. Didn't she think I could figure anything out?

Minutes later we were speeding up the hill toward the kennels.

"I hope you don't think I don't like your friends just because I was concerned about the party," Mom said, breaking the silence.

"No, I know."

"It's just . . . you've been so different here. You don't talk to me as much, and you spend a lot more time outside or in your bedroom or off with your friends."

I blew my hair out of my eyes. "Mom, you moved here so I could make friends and fit in, remember? Now you're freaking out because I'm so busy?"

Mom's lips twisted into a wry smile. "I know. Sounds silly, doesn't it?"

"Yeah."

"I don't know, though. I just sense an uneasiness or maybe a secretiveness in you that wasn't there before."

I fidgeted. God, what was she, a mind reader? "Mom, I'm sixteen, a teenager. What do you expect?"

Mom laughed and let it go. I relaxed in my seat. But what would Mom say when she found out about the fight Miller had got into? Our date and the party would vanish as though they had never existed.

Mom dropped me off and told me to call if I needed her. For what? Exercising the dogs? Ha! The mother hover was getting really old.

I took a deep breath when I walked into the kennels. I could almost feel my body relax. It was like a safe place, for both me and the dogs. I didn't have to impress anyone here.

The dogs went nuts when I walked in the door, and I hurried to feed them and clean their cages.

Laurie frisked about my legs when I went in to walk her. While I was attaching her leash to her collar, Aunt Shirley showed up, surprising me.

"Mind if I join you? Alan finished work early and is keeping the boys occupied so I can get out of the house."

"Sure."

Aunt Shirley put a halter onto one of the feisty black Labs, leaving its twin to cry foul in its cage. She laughed. "Don't worry, you're next."

We set off at a brisk pace. I hoped to get all the dogs walked by the time it got dark.

"Miller called and told me what happened," Aunt Shirley opened.

I grinned. "I knew you had a motive for coming out here with me."

"Well, there is that, too. But never underestimate a mother wanting to get away from her beloved offspring."

We walked in silence for a few minutes, stopping only when one of the dogs needed to relieve itself or sniff something.

"Do you want to tell me what happened?"

"Didn't Miller?" I asked, surprised.

"He told me about the fight and what started it, but not why this kid hates you so much."

"My friends and I saw him hitting on his girlfriend's sister. She's was a friend, so we told her."

"He sounds like a winner. Are you sure he was hitting on her?"

My shoulders twitched. "Yeah, he mentioned something

about them making out the night before. He and the sister, not his girlfriend."

"Really? Did everyone hear him?" Aunt Shirley's voice was leading and I decided I might as well fess up.

"No, actually, I read his lips," I admitted.

"Ahhh. So that explains his special hate of you in particular."

"Yeah."

We turned a corner and started back toward the barn.

"So I hear initiation starts next week."

I almost fell over and Aunt Shirley laughed.

"I grew up here, remember? And I'm not really that old. Are you excited or nervous?"

Relief washed over me. It would be nice to be able to talk about it with someone besides the girls. Someone who had some perspective. "Actually, I'm scared shitless."

Her lips curved into a remembering smile. "I felt the same way. But it's not that bad. I lived and so will you."

I snorted. "What about the girls who got hurt? When the administration banned exclusive organizations?"

Aunt Shirley frowned and her steps slowed. "That should have never happened. The initiations got out of hand. The girls mostly keep a handle on that now."

I could only hope.

She suddenly stopped and looked at me. "The alumnae are watching this group of girls pretty closely. Not everyone is happy with some of the things that are going on.

If the initiations do go too far, you need to tell me. I still know people."

There was that Godfather thing again. "So what did you do in the sorority?"

"I was the president."

My mouth fell open. She was pretty enough, but didn't look at all preppy anymore in her faded comfy jeans and old work boots.

Aunt Shirley laughed. "Believe it or not, I used to be pretty popular. Of course, the club ran a bit differently then. I mean, it had become more social than political, but it wasn't nearly as exclusive as it is now. Maybe girls are bitchier now than when I went to school."

I laughed and we walked for a minute in silence. I was hesitant to ask her what I was thinking, but I figured what the hell—there was no one else to ask. "Was everyone, like, the same, when you went to school? Like carbon copies of one another?"

She shrugged. "Yeah, I think it's part of living in a small town. I don't think you have to worry about that, though. I have a feeling you're an original."

I digested that for a moment. Was I? I felt sort of weird talking to Aunt Shirley this way. As if we'd been close for years. But it was kind of . . . nice.

"You have to be an original," she continued softly, "or else Miller wouldn't like you so much. He's had a hard time since his mom died and doesn't really relate well to people, but he certainly seems to open up to you."

I tingled down to my toes. "He seems to get along better with critters."

"That he does." She stopped and placed her hand onto my arm. "Be careful with Miller. I have a feeling you're actually stronger than he is in many ways."

I didn't answer because I had no idea what to say. I didn't feel that strong. In fact, I was beginning to feel like a puppet.

We finished walking the big dogs and let the little dogs into the puppy pens to run around.

"I've got to get back into the house and save my hubby from the kids." Aunt Shirley gave me a pat on the back and left me to my work.

I finished cleaning up the kennels, thinking the whole time. So Miller really did like me. Enough for people to notice. That was good. Then I remembered our fight and how he could hardly bring himself to tell me what had happened today. Would we ever be able to really get it together enough to have a relationship?

Aunt Shirley drove me home after I finished cleaning up. I'd hung around for a bit, hoping Miller would show up, but he never did. Patrice's car was in the driveway when we pulled up.

Why was I not surprised?

Aunt Shirley said something, but I didn't catch it.

"What was that?" I asked, opening the car door.

She faced me and grinned. "I said, speak of the devil. Just remember what I said. You have any problems with initiation week, you just let me know."

Nothing like having the Godfather in your corner.

Patrice was sitting in the living room with my mom. Mom hopped off the couch when I walked in. "I told you she'd be home in a few minutes. I'm going to go start dinner. Do you want to eat with us, Patrice?"

Patrice shook her head. She had her parent face on. "I have too much homework, but thank you very much."

Mom's mouth turned down in disappointment as she left the room. No wonder Patrice was first in everything. The way that chick wrapped people around her little finger was stellar.

She dropped her polite face and turned to me. "We need to talk."

I nodded. "Let's go to my room."

"This is fantastic," Patrice said when we reached my room. "Your mom is awesome."

I sat on the bed and waited. She hadn't come here to compliment my mom's decorating abilities.

She kicked off her shoes and sat down next to me. "You did okay at the interview today. Some of the girls aren't sure you should be in the sorority, but we made it."

We? She didn't have to worry—she was already in the sorority. I just nodded.

"I think you'll be great. I really do." Her voice was so

soft that I couldn't hear a word, but her lips said it perfectly. My throat closed and I was stupidly near tears.
Maybe she really did like me for me.

"So what news do you have for me?"

Or maybe not.

I sighed. "I told you that I had a little visit from Annie
and Meredith yesterday, right?" She nodded and my stomach
tightened. I hoped I wasn't signing my own death warrant
by telling her. "They wanted a favor from me. They want me
to spy on you and Sonya to help them choose which one will
be president next year."

"Those bitches," Patrice breathed. "How dare they?"

Like she'd forgotten she had asked me to do the same
thing to Sonya. I shrugged.

She gave a fierce scowl. "We'll just have to figure out a
way to turn the tables on them. Did you find anything out
on Sonya?"

I hesitated. "I'm not sure if it means anything."

"Spill it," she ordered. "I'll decide if it's important or
not."

I told her what Sonya had said to Kayla, leaving out the
part about Sonya sleeping with Scott. For all I knew she'd
made that up. But I did tell Patrice that Sonya was out to
get him.

"She is so going down."

The grim look on her face made me glad she was on my
side. *Note to self: Don't cross Patrice.*

Her face cleared. "You're just going to have to keep a closer eye on her. Especially at my party. I know Sonya—if she's going to try something, she's gonna want to flaunt it. Maybe we can trap her or something."

Patrice looked thoughtful as she lay back on the bed. Then she shot up. "Oh, hey, I almost forgot. What happened with the fight today?"

I rolled my eyes. "Seems like our boy Tyler found out it was me who sold him out. He called me a few unmentionable names and Miller jumped him."

She let out a big breath. "Shit. We're going to have to be careful about who finds out about your talents—otherwise they'll be useless."

And we wouldn't want that would we?

I was relieved when she left. Everything inside me had tied itself into knots and my stomach churned. I looked at myself in the mirror. Who was that chick with the pink T-shirt and designer jeans? Where was the dark eyeliner and black hoodie? Where was the screw-them-all attitude?

In a fit of defiance I seized a hoodie and yanked it on. I flung open my closet door and grabbed my board. It was dark out, but I didn't care. The streetlights would be enough. I needed to skate. Forget about secret sororities and fitting in and carbon copies. Tomorrow I would put on my costume and be who they wanted me to be, but right now I needed to be me again.

Eleven

The school day crawled by. My algebra teacher asked the class why we even bothered to have school before homecoming weekend. No one could answer him.

Too bad Miller couldn't be there. Of course, he wasn't interested in homecoming or school events. He was, however, interested in me. I hugged the conversation I'd had with my aunt to my heart and didn't tell Rachel or anyone. He liked me. Just the way I was. He knew about my insecurities and my deafness and everything. Still liked me. Amazing.

I glanced over at his empty desk while trying to ignore Ms. Fisher's boring lecture on the Cold War.

He'd called last night and told me about his job. He'd thought about me. So sweet. Of course, he hadn't mentioned the fight or the suspension. But I was getting used to his ways. At least he'd called.

The bell rang, cutting Ms. Fisher off in midbore. Thank God, the day was half over.

Rachel and I walked to lunch together. "You want me to come over and do your hair and stuff?" Rachel asked.

"What? No! It's not fancy, is it?"

Rachel must have seen the panic on my face, because she burst into laughter. "No, I just wondered if you wanted a makeover or something."

"Do I need one?" I asked, horrified at the thought.

"No!" Rachel shook her head. "It's supposed to be fun."

"Sounds like torture to me. Besides, he likes me the way I am."

Rachel smiled at me. "That's so nice."

"Don't you think Tim likes you the way you are?" Rachel had recently admitted a crush on a football player named Tim. I eyed Rachel's flawless skin and sky blue eyes. How could he not like her?

"I'm sure he does and he's a real sweetie, but at this point we're just friends."

"But he asked you to homecoming."

Rachel dimpled. "He so did. And I'll probably see him at the party tonight."

We picked up our lunches and walked over to the table. Kayla and Kelly were still sitting at opposite ends. Sonya and Patrice had obviously chosen sides—Sonya sat with Kayla and a quiet girl named Mandy, while Patrice sat next to Kelly. The group was dividing. Kayla would probably still have bruises for her homecoming pictures. Served her right.

Patrice poked me in the ribs. I choked on my mouthful of salad. "What? I'm trying to eat here."

"There's Mr. Bernard and Mrs. Weber. See what they're saying."

I stretched my neck, trying to see. "There's too many people in the way."

Patrice gave me a little push. "Well, go over there and see!"

"Okay, okay."

I got up and moved closer. I didn't look out of place because some students were having an impromptu pep rally in that part of the cafeteria. When I finally got into a position to see the teachers' mouths, I couldn't believe the changes that had taken place.

Instead of tense and unhappy, their expressions were relaxed. They weren't actually holding hands, but they might as well have been, because their glow was that obvious.

"When are you going to tell him?" Mr. Bernard asked.

"Next week, when he gets back from hunting. I'm so happy we are finally doing something," Mrs. Weber said.

Mr. Bernard smiled at her. "We couldn't —a baby on the way." His moustache made it hard to see what he said, but I got enough.

The two teachers wandered off. Holy crap! This was seriously scandalous! I headed back, feeling the sting of guilt. I was messing with people's lives. Maybe I should make something up?

Patrice sat drumming her fingers on the table. Sonya had scooted closer to her. Rachel looked up from her lunch expectantly.

Patrice leaned forward. "So? What's the scoop?"

"Where are Kayla and Kelly?" I asked, stalling for time.

Rachel raised her eyebrows. "They're out talking."

Sonya snorted. "More like they're trying to decide who gets Tyler."

"Who'd want him?" Rachel said.

Patrice sipped her soda and shoved her tray back. "I'd never date a guy I caught cheating on me."

Sonya's eyes narrowed. "Really?"

"Yup." Patrice gave her a cool look. "But before breaking it off, first I would murder him and the bitch he'd slept with." She leaned toward me. "Now spill, Serena. I wanna know the dirt on the songbird and the jock."

I bit my thumbnail. It wasn't as though I could just tell them no. I sighed. "She's leaving her husband."

"How romantic," Patrice said. "Star-crossed lovers and all that. Sorta."

Rachel clutched her throat and made gagging noises. "Ewww. They're teachers—they're old!"

"Anything else?" Patrice asked.

I hesitated.

"Maybe she's losing her touch," Sonya taunted.

I shot her a dirty look. "She's pregnant."

Mouths hung open all around me.

"That's super appalling," Patrice said.

"How do you know it's his?" Sonya asked.

I rolled my eyes. "I went up and asked them. Duh. I don't know. But they seemed too happy about it for it to be her husband's."

"Maybe her husband's shooting blanks?" Patrice suggested.

"Ewww!" Rachel made more gagging noises.

Patrice laughed. "Well?"

The bell rang, putting a stop to our discussion about our teachers' reproduction, though I knew that wouldn't be the end of it.

The rest of the day passed in a flash. Soon I was heading out the doors with hundreds of other kids excited for homecoming weekend. We had changed our plans slightly. Rachel and Patrice were going to pick me up for the game, and then everyone was heading home afterward to get ready for the party. Miller would pick me up there.

Last night had done me some good, I'd decided. I needed to skate more. I was actually more excited for the game than I thought I'd be, though I'd probably be too busy reading lips and spying to actually enjoy it. Bummer.

I raced home and ran upstairs to my room. I had to figure out something to wear. The sorority would be in full force tonight and I had to look good. Not to mention Miller and I would be having our first real date.

I looked through my wardrobe for something cool to wear. Not something preppy. The carbon copy remark still stung. But I didn't want to be stuck in just a T-shirt, either.

To my surprise I found a shirt with the tags still on it hanging in my closet. "Perfect," I breathed.

I held it up to my body in front of the mirror. Dark purple lace held together sheer light purple panels. The shirt flared out around my hips and tied with a dark purple ribbon just below my breasts. I looked down and saw a dark purple choker with a black disk attached to it sitting on my dresser. Matched with a pair of dark jeans, the shirt and choker would be perfectly me. Pretty and different, but still me. I could throw my school hoodie over my outfit for the game and then I'd be ready for the party way before Miller picked me up.

Wow. Maybe Mom does understand me after all.

I went downstairs and gave her a hug. "Thanks—they're awesome."

"I thought you'd like them. I really do want you to have fun, you know."

"It's going to be a blast. Miller can't go to the game because he's . . . working." God, I'd almost said "suspended." I *so* didn't want to open that can of worms, as she obviously hadn't spoken to Aunt Shirley about it yet. "But he's going to pick me up here after the game."

"Do you need a ride?" Mom asked.

"Nah, Rachel's got it covered."

I noticed a flash of red out front. "She's here. Gotta run." I gave her a kiss, which seemed to please her. Moms were as easy as skate guys.

The game passed in a blur. The only time anyone mentioned reading lips was when Meredith and Annie cornered me to find out if I had any dirt yet. I told them exactly what Patrice had told me to tell them—that Sonya was planning something, but I wasn't sure what. That seemed to satisfy them, and Patrice winked at me when I got back to the bleachers. Phew. We even won the game by a good margin, which was an added bonus.

I now stood in front of the mirror getting ready for my first real date. Making out at the skate park after school didn't count.

I was glad that I had been able to come home between the game and the party. Gave me time to fix my makeup and calm my nerves. Going to a party like this wasn't like hanging out at the skate park, either. Of course, the skate park was easier. I didn't have to spy on, like, a gazillion people at the same time. Maybe I'd take the night off and just enjoy being with Miller. I smiled at myself and ran a brush through my hair one last time.

I didn't want him to have to deal with the mother hover, so I ran downstairs early. Mom and Dad oohed and aahed, and even though it was cheesy, it still made me feel good.

The doorbell rang a few minutes after that and I opened the door, my heart pounding. What would he look like? Was he as excited as I was?

Something about the pained look on Miller's face told me no. We said good-bye to my parents and walked out to the truck.

To say I was disappointed would have been an understatement. Not even his reaching out to take my hand made it any better. "I take it you don't really want to go tonight?"

"No, I want to. I know how much it means to you."

I yanked my hand out of his. "Don't do me any favors. I wouldn't want to force you."

He sighed. "No, that came out wrong. I want to take you to the party. I want to be with you. I'm just not that great at parties."

I looked up into his eyes and my insides melted. Okay, I'd let him off the hook. He was so beautiful. I knew it was a weird thing to think about a guy, but it was true.

"We don't have to stay too long if you don't want to. I'm not that great at parties, either. Or maybe I am. I've never actually been," I admitted. "My old social life consisted of sneaking out to the skate park to hang out."

He smiled and opened the door for me. "Well, then let's go try it. At least we won't be alone if it turns out we both suck at it." He went around to his side, hopped into the truck, and pulled away from the house. "So what do you think it's going to be like tonight?"

I shrugged, even though I knew he couldn't see me in the dark. "I don't know. Patrice knows a lot of people. So it could be huge. Do you know how to get there?"

"Yeah, I went there when I was a kid. Her parents hosted some kind of class party thing for the second and third grades."

It always surprised me to be reminded that he'd lived here his whole life. Sometimes he seemed like more of an outsider than I was.

But then again, how much of an outsider would I be if I didn't read lips?

We ended up parking like a million miles away because of all the cars. Good thing I didn't like heels, I thought, hiking up a hill and around a corner.

I heard the music before I saw the house, and my stomach clenched in apprehension. The closer we got, the more I thought that maybe this wasn't such a good idea.

I stopped.

"Sure you want to do this?" he asked. "We could always go make out."

I couldn't see his face but I felt him laughing next to me.

I gave his arm a squeeze, admiring the muscles beneath my fingertips. "Let's leave that option open, shall we?" I took a deep breath. "Here we go!"

Twelve

I stopped again at the bottom of the driveway and clutched Miller's arm. "I'm going to have to turn my hearing aids way down, so I won't be able to hear anything. If you want to talk to me, you have to let me know, okay?"

"Sure. Are you going to be okay?"

The light of the streetlamp illuminated the concern in his eyes. I smiled. "I'll be fine." But I wasn't. I was terrified.

I didn't need my hearing aids to know how loud the music was. The bass rumbled in my stomach and chest. The house looked like a showplace. As the daughter of an interior decorator I could tell that it had been professionally done.

There must have been a hundred teenagers in the large living room and dining room beyond. Kids dotted the grand staircase and I could see more on the balcony above.

We threaded our way through the crowd, searching for Patrice or Rachel. Miller paused to talk to people several times. Some of the kids actually seemed glad to see him and his expression lightened. Patrice grabbed me up in a hug. She yelled something but I couldn't catch it.

"Don't yell!" I yelled back at her. "I can't read your lips!"

Patrice nodded and spoke normally. "Isn't this insane? Some of the kids brought alcohol, so watch it." She jerked her head toward Miller, who stood a couple of feet away talking to Tim.

"Like who?" I asked.

"Tyler."

Oh. I nodded.

"There's tons of food and some drinks by the fridge. I have to go make sure no one is getting out of hand. Remember, we're meeting up soon to give out initiation tasks for Monday."

She slipped off into the crowd and I grabbed sodas for Miller and me. At least it would keep my hands busy.

Tim went off to find Rachel. Miller led me out of the kitchen and we picked our way carefully up the stairs. My heart thudded in my chest, though I tried to keep my face normal. The panic of seeing so many people and not hearing anything overwhelmed me.

He turned and faced me. "I've heard about Patrice's pool table. Want to go find it?

I nodded and smiled, even though checking out of this madhouse and finding a quiet spot to make out was looking better and better.

The music wasn't as forceful upstairs and I turned my

hearing aids back up. We went into the game room and my jaw dropped. For a moment I forgot my anxiety. Ornate and beautifully constructed out of polished wood, the pool table looked as if the room had been built around it. Even the teenagers playing a game on it were treating it with proper respect.

"That's so tight!"

"Patrice's parents had it brought here from an old Southern mansion that was being condemned. It's almost two hundred years old."

Somebody bumped me and I jumped.

I watched Miller say something to the person, then he turned to me. "Are you okay?"

"I'm fine." I set my drink on a table. Someone grabbed me from behind and I jumped again. God, I was going to have to calm down or I'd ruin everything.

I turned and Rachel hugged me. She checked out my outfit. "You look fab!"

"Thanks—you too." When did Rachel *not* look fab?

Tim was with her, and he challenged Miller to a game as soon as the table was free.

Miller grinned. "I'm a shark," he warned.

Tim laughed. "I'm up for it. We gotta do something. The girls have been summoned."

I raised an eyebrow at Rachel and she nodded. "We're meeting the rest of the girls in the basement for a quick conference. I told Patrice I'd find you."

Miller and I glanced at each other. I didn't think either one of us wanted to be separated, but he gave me a quick nod.

I waved my hand. "Lead the way."

I followed Rachel downstairs, but she took me out onto the deck instead of to the basement.

She turned. "I wanted to warn you before we got down there. You were right."

I laughed. "I'm always right, dontcha know. What am I right about this time?"

"Sonya really is out to get you. She came and spoke to me about you, and I know she talked to some of the other initiates as well."

My stomach flip-flopped. "What did she say?"

"Just some shit about you not being sorority material and how you don't really seem all that interested. She even went so far as to say that someone got left out because you got in, which I know is total crap."

Did I really need this? Was being part of the A-list worth getting used and backstabbed? "Maybe Sonya's right—maybe I'm not sorority material."

"Don't say that!" Rachel reached out and gave my hand a squeeze. "You are totally sorority material and more. You're funny and original, which scares the crap out of girls like Sonya."

I gave her a surprised look. Maybe there was more to Rachel than her princess facade indicated.

"Plus, you have Patrice totally on your side, and the seniors seem to like you, too. Don't worry about it—you're in. Come on. We should get down there."

I followed her down to the basement. Even Patrice's basement wasn't a normal basement. It was a media room complete with a big-screen TV, a bar, and racks of stereo equipment. Her parents must make bank.

About twelve girls sat on the floor, some twirling their hair nervously around their fingers while others chewed on their fingernails. This was it. A few gave me dirty looks when I came in. They must be Sonya-ites.

Patrice stood up in front of the group and smiled. "I wish I could say that Sonya and I had a hard time choosing this year's recruits, but we didn't. You guys are obviously the cream of the crop. Congratulations on making it this far."

Annie walked over next to her. "A word of warning before we welcome this year's president. Initiation week is tough. It's how we weed out the A-listers from the losers." She paused, her eyes running over all of us with a steely gaze. "Not all of you are going to make it through initiation week."

"Oh, I don't know," Patrice put in mildly. "This is a great group of girls. Sonya and I were pretty careful." She turned. "Now, I'd like to welcome this year's president, Meredith Baxter."

Annie sat on the edge of the couch with Sonya as Meredith took center stage. Patrice darted upstairs, where the music still raged. Probably to make sure the house wasn't being torn apart.

"I agree with Patrice—you guys are awesome this year and I hope you all make it. Not that all of you will, but I can hope, right?" She gave us a wicked grin before continuing. "You all know the benefits of being in the sorority. Lifelong friends with the best people. Girls who will have your back for the rest of your life. Fun in the sun, parties, and loyalty are just a few of the things in store for you once you've made it past initiation week. This year we decided against going to Florida for spring break. Instead, get ready for margaritas and mojitos in Cabo!"

The girls cheered and I looked around. Would all their parents have the money for a trip like that? From the worried looks on a couple of faces, I thought not.

Meredith continued after the cheering had subsided. "I just wanted to go over some of the rules. There's a lot more, and you'll get a packet after you become an official member, but these are important for you to know before your week gets started.

"The number-one rule is no one tells a soul. Even if you don't make it into the sorority, you say nothing to no one. We have ways of making girls very, very sorry if they narc on us." She gave each of us a hard look before moving on. "Number two, if someone asks why you are doing the crazy things you'll be doing, you tell them that you lost a bet. Number three, if a sorority girl is in trouble, you do whatever you can to help them. If we don't have one another's back, then why even have a sorority? Very important. Number four, and this is a biggie, no one goes after a sorority sister's boyfriend unless she is already through with him."

Kelly glared at Kayla, who looked at the floor. Rachel stifled a giggle next to me and I grinned at her. I glanced over at Sonya and her eyes shifted away from me. *Interesting.*

Meredith wasn't through with us yet. "If any of these rules are broken, you go up before the council and will probably be kicked out of the sorority. So remember them. Annie, you have the shots ready?"

Annie was now behind the bar. Her short hair was askew and she looked as though she'd already started without us. She nodded and waved her hand at the countertop, which was lined with glasses.

"Okay, we have the envelopes with your first assignments," said Meredith. "The assignments will be rotated so not all of you will do the same thing every day. Don't open them till you get home, and destroy them after you read them, and remember, if you don't participate in every assignment, you'll automatically be kicked out." She gave a big smile. "Now let's seal that with a shot!"

We lined up single file at the bar where Sonya handed everyone a small pink envelope and a shot of tequila.

"And I told my parents there would be no alcohol," I murmured to Rachel, who was behind me in line.

She giggled. "I have gum."

When I got up to the bar Sonya winked at me and handed me an envelope. "I got a special assignment just for you." She handed me a shot. "Drink up, Serena. Celebrate your initiation week!"

"Thanks, Sonya—I knew you'd be thinking of me." I tossed the burning liquid down my throat and my eyes watered. Warm beer was the extent of my drinking experience. Tequila was obviously a whole different ball game. I slipped the envelope into the back pocket of my jeans.

While I waited for Rachel to be done with her shot, I noticed Meredith and Annie looking all the initiates up and down as they walked by and making notes on a clipboard. Every once in a while they would whisper to each other and giggle. My stomach tightened.

Rachel came up to me, still coughing from her shot.

I pointed to them. "What's up with that? They judging our clothing or what?"

Rachel shook her head. "Nah, they're just trying to be as intimidating as possible. Let's go find our men," she said, putting her arm through mine.

I tried not to wonder what they were writing down about me as we made our way through the gauntlet. Then I turned my hearing aids back down. Patrice caught us when we got to the first floor.

"I'm so excited," she said. "I can't wait till you guys are full members."

"One more week," Rachel said.

Patrice nodded and opened her mouth to say something when she noticed an accident across the room. "No, don't wipe it up! I'll get it!" She flashed us a smile. "Gotta run. If you see Scott, tell him I'm looking for him. I need him to help me get rid of some drunks before my parents get home." She hurried away.

The guys were still shooting pool when we got up to the game room, and I surprised Miller and myself by going up behind him and slipping my arms around his waist. "Having fun?"

He smiled down at me. "I missed you."

The warmth from the tequila had spread throughout my chest, and my legs were buzzing. Confidence hummed through my body along with the liquor. Screw Sonya. I suddenly wanted to get Miller alone before it wore off.

"You wanna take off?" I whispered.

His eyes glowed at me and his mouth twisted into a smile. "What did they do down there?" he asked Tim. "Get our women drunk?"

Rachel laughed and Tim flashed a smile. "We're better off not knowing, dude," he said.

"Let me finish this game first, okay?" Miller asked, and I nodded.

Rachel and I kicked back on a big couch and she handed me a piece of gum. Miller and Tim were evenly matched and it was a good game. I finished my soda and watched the guys play, then turned to Rachel.

"Is there a bathroom up here?" I so didn't want to have to go to the bathroom while kissing Miller.

"Yeah, it's one of those doors down the hall."

"Thanks."

I wandered down the hall, avoiding couples in midclutch. One door led to a closet and another one opened into an empty bedroom.

"Third time's the charm," I muttered, opening a door and flicking on a light.

A couple on the bed leaped up and the girl turned to button her shirt. The guy grinned.

"Hey, look. It's deaf girl," Scott said.

The girl turned, her eyes wide with shock. Sonya.

I backed out the door.

Her face hardened. "Read my lips, Serena. You say a word to Patrice and you'll be sorry. You got it? I'll make you sorry."

I turned and fled back to the pool room. Rachel and Tim were gone. I grabbed Miller by the hand. "Let's go."

He didn't question me, just followed as I led the way downstairs.

I worked my way through the crowd toward the door, running right into my favorite person. "Well, look who we have here," Tyler said, considering me and weaving on his feet. "I've got a score to settle with you, big mouth. Or maybe I should call you big eyes."

Tyler laughed at his own joke. Miller moved in front of me and said something to Tyler.

"I don't think so. I owe the bi—"

Miller hit him hard in the jaw, causing Tyler to fall back into the crowd. Miller advanced on him, but I grabbed his arm. "He's not worth it—come on!"

Miller looked at Tyler, who lay on the floor, his head lolling back, and he turned and followed me out the door.

We walked back down the hill without saying a word. I reached up and flicked the sound for my hearing aids back up before climbing into the truck.

"You know," I said, reaching out and clasping his hand, "I don't think I'm really a party person."

He shook his head. "That's okay. Me neither."

He turned the truck around and headed up a street I'd never been on. Of course, it was too dark to really tell.

"Where are we going?" I asked.

"A spot I know of." His voice was casual, but his nerves showed in the way he gripped the steering wheel.

I grinned, excitement lacing my stomach. "And what do you intend on doing at this spot?" I asked, teasing him.

"What we should have done in the first place," he growled. He glanced over at me. "You're sitting too far away. There's a seat belt in the middle, you know."

I scootched over next to him and he rewarded me by placing his hand on my leg. I shivered in spite of the heat his hand generated.

He parked the car and held out his arms, and I lay back across his lap. He folded me up in his arms and I laid my head against him. He smelled so good and I did what I had wanted to do the first time I got close to him—I leaned in and sniffed. Then I nibbled on his throat for good measure. His lips found mine, igniting little sparks that traveled from my mouth to my chest. I'd never been kissed like that. His kisses—long, slow, and sweet—made me feel loved. These kisses had nothing to do with the fast, sloppy kisses I'd had before. This was a whole new level of kiss. The superkiss, the megakiss, a kiss of stratospheric magnitude.

I didn't know how long we'd been kissing before Miller came up for air. He murmured something against my hair, but I didn't catch it.

"What was that?" I asked. He reached out and turned on the dome light, and I blinked.

He pulled away and looked into my eyes. "I said, I haven't been this happy in a very, very long time."

I knew he meant since his mom had died, and I ran my fingers down his jawline. "I'm glad. You make me happy, too. You make me feel normal."

"You are far from normal." He leaned forward and brushed his lips against mine. "You are wonderful and small and soft and perfect." He grabbed my hip, and I jumped a little and laughed.

"I'm *so* not perfect," I told him. "But you aren't either. You are stubborn and bullheaded, and you keep running away from me." I punctuated each word with a kiss against his neck. "But I like you a lot anyway."

He laughed and pulled me close. He kissed me again, his hand running its way down my leg. I pressed against him even more until he pushed me back into a sitting position next to him.

"I need to take you home."

His kisses made me disoriented and fuzzy. "Why?"

He gave me a look that curled my toes. "Because it's almost your curfew. Besides, it would be safer." He reached out with one arm and wiped the steam off the windshield.

"You don't scare me," I teased, and he squeezed my leg in reply.

We were home in minutes, and I skipped into the house after a final good-night kiss. In spite of Sonya, the sorority, and the spying, I didn't think I had ever been happier in my life.

The house was dark and I locked the door behind me. I snuck upstairs and then saw the light coming from under my parents' door.

I knocked before opening it and poking my head through. "I'm home."

"Did you have a good time?" Mom asked.

"I had a blast. I'll tell you about it in the morning."

"Okay." Mom set down her book and yawned. Dad snored on the other side of her. "Night, hon."

I tiptoed to my bedroom and flicked on the light. I pulled out the pink envelope from the back of my jeans. No time like the present.

Your assignment: Come to Jerry's Monday
afternoon wearing your bra and underwear
on the outside of your clothes. Welcome to
the club!

They had to be kidding. My face heated just thinking
about it. This had the mark of Sonya all over it.

I sighed and set the envelope and paper on my desk.
After changing into my nightgown, I crawled into bed and
read it again. I guessed a trip to Victoria's Secret was in
order. Mom would just love that.

I lay back against my pillows and turned out my light. I
wondered if they'd get pissed if I wrote SONYA SUCKS BUTT on
the rear end of my underwear.

Thirteen

The french fries in front of me tasted like cardboard, the kind that has been used to soak up oil in a second-rate auto shop. I bit into one anyway and methodically chewed and swallowed. The urge to gag overwhelmed me and I took a quick drink of soda. Then I slowly picked up another fry. Maybe if I ate them very slowly, my hour would be up about the same time the fries were gone.

My black and orange bra and underwear set from Victoria's Secret glowed like a neon sign. I had bought it hoping to blend in with the decor at Jerry's. Instead I looked like I was celebrating Halloween early.

The titters from around the restaurant told me that no one else was buying it, either. I think everyone from every high school in a three-hundred-mile radius had shown up today. Just my luck.

I bit into another tasteless fry and thought black thoughts

about Sonya. The object of my hatred had gone around to every table in the place and pointed me out. Her e-mail last night informed me I had to endure this humiliation for an hour. Before that I'd figured I'd be in and out in a matter of minutes.

Yeah right. I narrowed my eyes and looked around the restaurant. Shouldn't there be a few other lingerie losers strewn around the place? I knew we were doing our assignments in shifts, but this was ridiculous. My face flamed as another group of kids noticed my outfit. All those years enduring the taunts of other kids couldn't have prepared me for the sickness I felt at that moment.

I stared at my plate.

Someone said something, but I was too busy concentrating on *not* listening that I missed it. I glanced up. Darcy Freeman stood above me, her arms crossed and sympathy etched onto her face.

"What?" I asked.

"I said, is this worth it?"

"At the moment, no." I indicated the seat across from me. "Want to share in the fun?"

She sat and shook her head. "You have a very strange idea of fun."

I shrugged. "Maybe I get off on utter humiliation."

She shook her head. "Nah, I think you just want to belong."

My stomach tightened, though I didn't think it could feel any worse. "Who doesn't?" I challenged.

She stared at me a moment and then started to giggle. "Me, obviously."

I gave her a reluctant smile. "Oh, right."

Her blue eyes zeroed in on me, all the laughter gone. "I bet you heard I blew the interview, didn't you?"

I shifted in my seat and couldn't meet her eyes.

She snorted. "I thought so. It isn't true, you know."

"It's not?"

She shook her head and reached out to grab one of my fries. "I know that's what they tell everyone, but the truth is, I told them to stick it."

My confusion must have shown on my face, because she continued.

"Don't believe me? Why? Because what girl in her right mind wouldn't want to be in their little secret sorority? How many girls do you think are actually in it? Altogether?"

I shook my head. "I dunno."

"I'm thinking thirty-five, maybe forty. And there are hundreds of girls at school who aren't in it."

I sat back and digested that.

"Bet you thought it was the end-all and be-all of your life, huh?"

"No!" I lied.

She gave me a superior look. "Sure ya did. You want to know why I told them no?"

I nodded. If nothing else, the time I had to sit there

displaying my underwear was going by faster with someone to talk to.

Darcy nabbed another fry. "Because my great-aunt was in the sorority when it first began, and let me tell you, it was nothing like it is now. It used to mean something. They did things like have sit-ins to protest sexism in the school, like unequal funding for programs or unfair dress codes. You wanna know what pisses off the sorority now? When the local mall runs short on Juicy Couture."

My face flushed recalling Kelly and Patrice having that very conversation.

Darcy gave a knowing laugh and jumped up. "Sure, all the It girls are in the sorority, but who wants to be an It girl when you could be out doing it? Living life. Getting an education. Making a real difference." Her eyes ran up and down my outfit. "You have to make up your own mind, but you don't strike me as an A-lister. 'Course, that's up to you. Now I had better get outta here before Sonya kills us both. Thanks for the fries."

I turned and caught Sonya's glare. Great.

Darcy sauntered off, leaving me to stare at her in disbelief. I tried to tell myself that she was just bitter, but that didn't explain all of it. She had too much confidence. Somehow I felt a lot more foolish sitting there in my bra and underwear now than before she'd arrived.

I glanced at my cell phone and sighed. Fifteen more minutes and I was outta there. I tried to digest what Darcy had told me, but I wasn't any more successful than I had been digesting the fries. Something about sitting there in my bra and underwear made thinking kinda tough.

I caught a glimpse of Kayla at the counter and giggled. 'Bout time. She wore a lacy green and pink thong and bra. Guess I wasn't the only one who had made a trip to Victoria's Secret over the weekend. How cute. It matched the green bruise on her eye.

Even though sitting with Kayla wasn't my idea of a good time, beggars couldn't be choosers. I tried to catch her eye to have her join me. I saw her wave to Sonya, who laughed and waved back. Then she paid for her soda and turned around and walked out.

What the hell?

I turned to Sonya, who smirked. Before I could react, Patrice walked in and came over to my booth.

Her eyebrows disappeared behind her bangs. "What are you doing? You enjoy being out in your underwear?"

I stared at her, horror knotting inside my chest. "What do you mean?"

"All you had to do was walk in, order something, and leave. You didn't have to sit here." She looked at my outfit. "Cute bra, by the way."

I glanced back at Sonya, who leered at me and waved. My fingers itched to hurl my soda at her. Why was she doing this to me? I wasn't hurting her. Why was I such a threat? Was it the lipreading? Or did she just hate me because I was deaf? Tears rose up behind my eyes.

Patrice must have caught my look and she turned. Sonya's eyes shifted to Patrice and challenged her from across the room.

Patrice turned back to me. "She did this, didn't she?"

I nodded. "She sent me an e-mail saying I had to stay an hour."

Patrice's face hardened. "Game is *so* on."

She grabbed my book bag and pulled me up by one arm. "Come on, I'll give you a ride home. How did you get here?"

"I walked."

Patrice led me out of the restaurant, pausing only long enough to give Sonya the glare of evil. I concentrated on holding back my tears.

Once in the car I slipped off my bra and underwear and put them into my backpack. Patrice was busy ranting and was definitely loud enough to hear.

"I am going to crucify that bitch! She can't just adjust the assignments for her own personal revenge." She gave me a sidelong glance. "That's how those girls got hurt. Someone messed with the system to drive an enemy out." Patrice hit her hand on the steering wheel. "If she thinks she's going to get that presidency, she's got another think coming. Do you still have the e-mail she sent?"

I shook my head. "I deleted it like I was supposed to. I didn't even save a draft."

"Crap. I could go to the board about today's little escapade, but I'm not sure they'd do anything in the middle of initiation week. Okay, did you get any information at the party?"

I stayed silent. I hadn't told her about what I'd seen. Saturday had been the homecoming dance and Mom and I had spent Sunday at the mall. Patrice pulled up in front of my house and I still hadn't said anything.

Finally I couldn't stand it. I owed her. She'd saved me and was proving to be a real friend. At least, most of the time.

"I saw them," I told her quietly. "I saw Sonya and Scott in bed together."

Patrice swallowed, tried to speak, and then swallowed again. Tears filled her eyes. "That jerk! He was so sweet to me at homecoming. And all the while he was boinking Sonya behind my back." She took a deep, shuddering breath. "Did they see you?"

I nodded. "Sonya threatened me if I told you."

She remained silent. I reached out and touched her arm. "You're better off without him. He's an ass."

She gave a watery smile and took another breath. "You're right. But Sonya is gonna pay. I'm going to the rest of the board and getting her removed, if I can." She glanced at me. "And I want to approve all your assignments from here on out, okay?"

I opened the car door. "Thanks. And thanks for the ride and, well, stuff."

Patrice nodded and drove off.

I spent the rest of the evening working at the shelter, then doing my homework. I kept one eye on my e-mail while I worked, waiting for tomorrow's assignment. But I couldn't get Darcy Freeman out of my mind. I used to think I had courage. That I was an original. Turns out, not so much. Everything I was doing felt . . . wrong. I wanted to talk to Miller but he was working late. Plus, he didn't know about all my spying. Rachel, as sweet as she was, wouldn't really understand.

My e-mail pinged. Oh, goody. I had mail.

Let's see you beg to get into the sorority!
Bring some old clothes to school tomorrow
because we'll be dropping you off downtown
to beg on a street corner. Have fun!!!

I took a deep breath. Reduced to begging. What the hell had I gotten myself into?

I sent it to Patrice and then pulled my paint clothes out of my closet. They were certainly grubbier than all the other new clothes that packed my closet.

I looked at myself in the mirror. Why was I doing this, again? Oh, right. To get friends. Maybe Darcy wasn't so far off after all.

I asked myself the same thing the next morning when I saw Meredith and Annie coming toward me.

Already? I hadn't even been at school for ten minutes yet.

Both wore somber business expressions. I sighed. I didn't quite say, "What now?" but I was thinking it.

There were no pleasantries this time.

"Are you sure it was Sonya you saw with Scott Friday night?"

Duh. "Considering the oh-so-pleasant conversation we had when I busted her, during which she threatened my ass, yeah, I'm positive."

Annie and Meredith glanced at each other. "This is serious," Meredith said. "But I'm not sure what we can do about it right now. You're the only one who saw it, and since you're not a member yet . . ." Her words trailed off and she shrugged.

Okay, now they were pissing me off. "That doesn't make sense," I told them. "You asked me to spy for you so you can figure out who you want to be president, and now you can't use the information?"

Annie shook her head. "No, we meant we can't kick her out of the sorority because of this, at least not till we have more proof. But there's no way she's getting the presidency."

"So she's not going to be president next year?" I asked. Membership in the sorority had just got more attractive.

"No. We'll probably talk to her during lunch, so don't say anything to anybody," said Meredith.

"Does Patrice know?"

Meredith nodded, but the late bell rang before she could say anything else.

"Good luck today," Annie said as they hurried off.

Yeah—when Sonya found out she wasn't going to be president next year because of me, I was gonna need it.

I wished Miller were around, but he wouldn't be back to school until the next day. My first three classes passed without incident, and I looked forward to lunch as much as I would a major hearing-aid malfunction. In other words, I'd almost rather die.

To my relief neither Sonya nor Patrice was present.

Kayla looked around. "I wonder what's up? They're usually all over the sophomores during initiation week."

Rachel cast a glance my way but said nothing. How much did she know?

"What's your assignment today?" Kelly directed the question at her sister, probably the first time she'd spoken to her freely since the Tyler incident.

Kayla leaned forward, obviously eager to make up. "I get to be a beggar today. What about you?"

"I get to show off my new Victoria's Secret stuff," Kelly said glumly.

Rachel laughed. "You went and bought new underwear, too?"

I snickered. "Me three."

Two other initiates at the end of the table chorused in that they, too, had gone out and bought new underwear.

We laughed together, dispelling some of the tension we'd been under since the night of the party.

I sighed. "Problem is, I'm not sure I can wear them again without remembering."

Rachel grimaced. "That bad, huh? No, don't tell me. Today's my day. Plus, we aren't supposed to talk about it."

Kayla shrugged. "I don't see any juniors or seniors, do you? That's what they get for leaving us alone."

"You want to go over together?" Kelly asked Rachel.

She nodded. "Humiliation loves company."

Kayla turned to me. "You're begging, too, right? Where do you think they're going to take us?"

It was the friendliest she'd ever been to me. Maybe she wasn't half bad away from Sonya.

I shrugged. "Not sure. Probably someplace that has the most people."

"I'll meet you after school by the front steps?" She gave me a tentative smile and I nodded.

"Sounds good to me."

My afternoon classes passed quickly, and before I knew it, I was filing and making copies in the office.

I was bent over the *L*s when I saw Mrs. Watson looking through the hall passes. The deep frown on her face showed her confusion.

She turned to me. "SERENA? DID YOU HAPPEN TO SEE WHAT I DID WITH THE EXTRA HALL PASSES? I COULD HAVE SWORN I MADE MORE THAN THIS BEFORE I WAS SICK LAST WEEK."

Cold flashed over me. I tried to say something, but no

noise came out. I coughed instead and then found my voice.

"No, Mrs. Watson. I haven't seen them."

"ARE YOU GETTING A COLD, DEAR? I HAVE SOME LEMON DROPS AROUND HERE SOMEWHERE." She pulled a bag out of her drawer and handed me one. Maybe I'd distracted her enough.

No such luck.

"MAYBE I MISCOUNTED."

She picked up some papers and went back to her work, leaving me in a puddle of apprehension. That had been a close one. Hopefully she wouldn't figure it out. For the first time I wondered if there were cameras in the office.

By the time the bell rang, I was a nervous wreck. I was so not looking forward to my street-corner assignment. We were just lucky they hadn't tried to tart us up like prostitutes. I wouldn't have put it past them.

I quickly changed into my paint clothes in the girls' bathroom and then hurried to where I was to meet Kayla and whoever was taking us to our location.

Kayla gave me a pained smile. "Hey."

No fair. Kayla's torn jeans and shirt made her look like Barbie slumming. I looked like a homeless person.

Another girl, Mandy, joined us on the steps. She smiled at us nervously.

"Any idea how long we have to do this?" I asked.

Kayla shook her head. "Who knows? We might have to walk home."

Patrice's car pulled up to the steps and I breathed a sigh of relief, thankful it wasn't Sonya.

"Hop in," she said, leaning over and opening the front door of her car.

We didn't have to be told twice.

She handed me a small can. "Here, put this on your face."

I looked at the label. Shoe polish. "They still sell this stuff?"

Patrice laughed. "I got it at the little shoe place downtown. I think it's the first thing the poor guy has sold in years. Be careful. Don't get any on my seats."

I rubbed liberal amounts of the slimy stuff on my face and handed it back to Kayla and Mandy.

Patrice grinned. "You guys look horrible! Wipe your hands off on the front of your shirts. We want you to look as poor as possible."

She pulled into a parking space close to one of the busiest intersections in town. Right near the veterinary hospital where Miller worked. I cringed. Patrice handed each of us an old can.

"Now, when someone comes up to you, you have to say, 'Alms, alms for the poor,' and hold out your can. Got it?"

We nodded.

"What are we supposed to do if someone gives us money?" Kayla asked.

"Save it," Patrice answered. Her eyes met mine. "We're giving all the money we collect to the no-kill shelter."

I gave her a slight smile and opened my car door. At least I'd be begging for a good cause. I'd have to remember that when people spit on me.

"I'll come and get you when you're done. I'll be parked where I can see you, so no trying to sneak off! Have fun!" I could see her laughing as she drove away.

"I think she's enjoying this way too much," Mandy said.

Kayla nodded and got her can ready as someone came walking up. "Payback for having to do this last year, probably." She walked toward the woman, who tried to shy around her. "Alms? Alms for the poor?"

The woman practically ran in the other direction and I laughed. "I take it there's not too many beggars in this town."

I readied myself as another person approached. "Alms? Alms for the poor?"

The man tossed some change into my can and I giggled. "I bet I get more than you guys."

Kayla laughed. "You're on!"

By the time a half an hour had passed, we were working that corner like professionals, sometimes racing one another toward a particularly well-dressed person. We counted up our money when no one was around. Maybe they'd meant for us to be humiliated, but we were actually having fun.

I saw another person farther down the sidewalk walking toward us. "I got this one!" I laughed over my shoulder, racing toward him.

My feet slowed when I saw who it was. Miller walked toward me holding a sheet of white paper. I tried to smile, but froze at the stormy expression on his face.

"Care to explain this?" he asked. "But I guess you don't really have to." He glanced at my clothes and face. "This tells me everything. I knew you wanted to be in that stupid sorority, but I had no clue you would stoop so low."

My stomach filled forebodingly. "I don't know what you're talking about. You already knew I wanted to be in the sorority. This is just part of initiation. I'm collecting money for a good cause," I said, holding the can of coins toward him. "It all goes to the shelter."

"Was I just a part of your little initiation?" He shoved the paper at me.

"No. How could you be . . . ? I mean . . ." I looked at the paper and gasped as the title stared up at me. *Read My Lips*.

"That's what I mean," he bit out, his lips tight. "Stay away from me, Serena. I don't want anything to do with you. Do you hear me? Nothing."

He turned to walk away and I grabbed his sleeve.

"Miller! Wait!" He shrugged me off and rushed back toward the vet's office.

I looked down at the paper again, but tears made the words all blurry.

But I knew one thing. Whatever it was, there could be only one explanation: Sonya.

Fourteen

I stood in shock looking after him. The piece of paper he'd handed me fluttered in the wind. I wiped my eyes on my sleeve and tried to read it, but I was still crying too hard to see.

Kayla came up and put her hand on my shoulder.

"What happened? What is that?"

She gently took the paper out of my hand and glanced at it. "Oh, shit. This is bad." She waved it around in the direction Patrice had gone and minutes later Patrice showed up.

"What's wrong? What's happened?"

I shook my head. I still hadn't moved. I wiped my eyes again while Kayla handed her the paper. Patrice held it while we all scanned the page.

READ MY LIPS
THE GOSSIP GIRL HAS NOTHING ON HILLSDALE HIGH'S LATEST SCANDAL DIVA!
CHECK OUT THE LITTLE TIDBITS SHE'S DISCOVERED SINCE THE YEAR BEGAN!

* What antismoking administrator has been seen smoking again?

* What teacher was surprised to have so many students prepared for a sneak pop quiz? Spies tell us it's because the Scandal Diva saw the teacher talking about it and proceeded to tell her classmates. Our diva performed a public service by warning others of what was coming!

* What songbird teacher has been busted for having an affair with what physically fit teacher? We hear congratulations are in order—they are expecting their first baby! What will the songbird's husband say? Tsk, tsk, tsk!

* Remember the fight between two formally close sisters at our favorite restaurant? Sources say our sharp-eyed Scandal Diva was intimately involved in that breakup. She sure gets around, doesn't she?

* What buff football hero won't be graduating with his class this year and may even have to turn down a scholarship? Just ask our resident scandal monger! Rumor has it that she saw the whole thing and then proceeded tell the entire school!

* Spreading gossip isn't the only profession Scandal Diva excels at. Lifting hall passes out of the office seems to be another talent. Bad girl!

* What rugged loner type has been seen smooching what new girl? So sad the loner doesn't know it's all a farce.

Turns out new girl had to go out with him to get into a secret sorority! Now that she's close to getting in, how long will it take before she dumps him back into the white-trash Dumpster where he belongs?

"I think I'm going to throw up," I mumbled. Patrice led me over to a bench and sat down with me.

"Breathe," she ordered, looking over the paper again.

Easier said than done. My breath was coming out in little gasps and my throat closed every time I tried to pull in more oxygen. Probably couldn't make it past the lump of tears and fear that had lodged itself in my throat.

I tried not to let the panic that fluttered in my chest take over. All gone. My life here had just disappeared in a puff of smoke. Everyone would know I was the Scandal Diva, wouldn't they? Oh, gawd. Miller. Not only did he think that I'd gone after him because of the sorority, but he'd found out I'd been spying on people.

I looked from Patrice to Kayla. Mandy stood a few feet away, unsure of what to do. I finally spoke up. "Do you think Sonya passed this around school? Do you think people will know that I was the one who did all that? Will they think I wrote this?"

Patrice studied the handout. "I think we can expect that kids will now know everything. Sonya might leave these lying around at Jerry's. She was really clever using 'saw' instead of 'overheard,' huh? And again here"—Patrice pointed to another item—"she also used 'sharp-eyed.' Not to mention the title of the whole thing—it's pretty incriminating. But remember, finding out about gossip isn't against school policy. Spreading it in print is. It would be considered slander, although the administration would never be able to prove Sonya made this kind of handout."

"But this was a perfect way to really stick the knife into you, Serena," Patrice continued. "Sonya knew that Miller and you were going out. Plus, look at the item about you stealing the hall passes." She shook her head. "She saw the hall passes when I was getting something out of my notebook and guessed. I don't think it's going to matter who spreads this around. People are going to know it was you who did all this."

"Oh, gawd. Everyone is going to hate me."

I began to shake and couldn't stop. So cold. Why was I so cold? "What am I gonna do? My parents are going to kill me."

"Don't do anything. Come to school tomorrow like normal. I'm going to take this to the sorority board. Sonya made a huge mistake when she mentioned the sorority. That is taboo at any time." Patrice put her arm around me and squeezed. "We'll figure something out."

Right now I couldn't have cared less about the stupid sorority. I wished I'd never even heard of it. I just wanted to know what Patrice and the rest of them were going to do to save my ass from getting kicked out of school. The hall passes alone could get me suspended.

Patrice dropped me off at my house after we'd stopped at a gas station so we could wash off and change our clothes. I slipped upstairs without talking to Mom. I didn't want to face her.

Once in my room I threw myself down onto my bed. The sketch Miller had done mocked me from the wall. What was I going to do?

I didn't know how long I had been lying there on my bed when the flash of my cell phone caught my attention. A text from Rachel.

I need you to meet me at my house. Big meeting going on.

Hope started building in my chest. Maybe they'd figured something out?

I ran downstairs and asked Mom for a ride. If she noticed anything wrong, she didn't mention it.

There were several cars in front of Rachel's spacious home, but I didn't see Patrice's.

Rachel was waiting for me and the door swung open before I could knock.

"Come on, we're all up in my bedroom." She led me upstairs.

Her room was packed with girls, including Kelly and Kayla. Most of them I recognized from the party. Each one held a piece of paper. My heart sank. It was *the* piece of paper. Sonya hadn't wasted any time.

Rachel sat on the bed and patted a spot next to her. "I got these from Jerry's when I was there for my assignment.

I filled everyone else in on what has been happening."

I nodded. So? Like that would help me at all.

Rachel continued. "Sonya set up a website. It's basically just the same thing she has here. I got all the initiates to come over so we can figure out what we're going to do."

My throat tightened. Rachel was a real friend. But what *could* we do?

One of the girls held up the paper and looked at me. "This isn't fair. They practically forced you to do this for them and then they turned on you."

I shook my head. "They didn't force me, really—I could have said no."

Kelly snorted. "Like anyone can say no to Patrice or Sonya."

A couple of the other girls nodded in agreement.

"Yeah, they're pretty persuasive," Mandy said.

Rachel nodded. "I was there most of the time, and while Serena wasn't actually forced, she had very little choice. The question is, what are we going to do about it? Now word is that Sonya isn't going to be the president next year. She may even get kicked out." Rachel patted my hand. "I got that from Patrice."

"What can we do about it?" one dark-haired girl asked. "We don't really have any power in the sorority or in the school."

Rachel shook her head. "We have more power than we think. How many of us are being asked into the sorority because we have relatives who were in it?"

A little over half the girls raised their hands.

Rachel smiled. "We have alumnae power. Also, where would the sorority be if it had no recruits? If this entire year was a bust because they couldn't get anyone to join?"

My admiration for Rachel grew. She was *so* not the naive princess I thought she was.

I looked at the girls, some of whom had turned pale at the thought of standing up to the sorority.

Rachel looked hard at each girl. "My thought is that we boycott the assignments tomorrow. That will get our point across that they are going to have to do something about this mess."

Kelly raised her hand. "What good would that do? Wouldn't we all get kicked out?"

Rachel shook her head. "I don't think so. Not only do they need us for the sorority to continue, but we would be displaying one of the sorority virtues—watching a sorority sister's back."

One of the girls who had raised her hand about having a relative in the sorority spoke up. "The sorority didn't used to be like this. My mom told me that it was started during the women's rights movement and anyone could join."

Another girl agreed. "Yeah. Now it doesn't do anything but establish you as a popular girl. And if they can do this to Serena, what's to stop them from doing this to any of us?"

I swallowed hard, watching these girls stick up for me. I

belonged. I really and truly belonged. Maybe not the way I'd pictured it, but I still had friends.

"I don't want anyone to risk themselves for me," I broke in. "If any one of you wants to back out of the boycott, just say so."

Kayla raised her hand, looking apologetic. "I'm not sure I want to."

Kelly slammed her sister's hand down. "You owe me, and I say you're doing this if you want to continue to be my twin."

Kayla looked at her for a second and then nodded. "I'm in."

Rachel grinned. "Good! The other thing we have to do is, those of us who have alumnae connections need to clue them in. The board wouldn't think about going against all those women. Especially not since so many of the seniors are going to be pledging to various college sororities next year or trying to get jobs."

"That won't help me with the administration, though," I said glumly.

Rachel wrinkled her nose at me and smiled. "You might be surprised."

The meeting broke up after we agreed to meet at Jerry's after school the next day. We thought it would be more effective if the board knew right off the bat that we were boycotting.

Rachel grabbed my arm. "Wait here. I'll give you a ride home."

I nodded and she walked the other girls out. She came back a few minutes later.

"I talked to Patrice," she said. "But I didn't tell her about the meeting tonight. It wouldn't have been fair to tell her stuff she couldn't tell the rest of the board members. She feels really bad about what happened."

I sighed. "The worst part of it is Miller. He wouldn't even talk to me."

She pulled me up off the bed. "Don't worry about it. He'll realize that you wouldn't do that when he cools off."

My throat tightened. "Maybe."

Then again, maybe not. He was so stubborn. And especially with all the secret spying I'd been doing. Something told me Miller wouldn't like that at all.

Rachel dropped me off at my house. Mom asked me if I wanted to go to the shelter and gave me a strange look when I said no. I probably should have so I could have talked to Aunt Shirley, but somehow I couldn't see myself doing that. I would have had to admit too much, and even though I knew it was all going to come out eventually, I wasn't ready to talk about it. Besides, I really didn't want to run into Miller. All I wanted to do was go to bed.

I knew the minute I walked into school the next day that word had spread. Pieces of white paper flooded the hallways. I had to give Sonya credit. When she did something, she did it up good.

The morning passed in a haze. Everywhere I went, people were laughing and giggling over the flyer. Some students actually came right out and asked me if I was the Scandal Diva. I was tempted to turn off my hearing aids and ignore everybody.

My stomach turned as I walked into American history. Ms. Fisher glared as I went to my desk.

"Hey, Miller," I saw someone yell from the back. "Been dumped into the Dumpster yet?"

Miller stared straight ahead. The crimson of his cheeks was the only sign that he'd heard the mocking comment.

I stared at my desk, my heart in my throat.

"That's enough of that," Ms. Fisher said. She stood leaning on her desk. She looked at the class for a long moment, letting her gaze linger on me.

"It has come to my attention that some of our students knew about the last pop quiz before it happened. That gave them an advantage over those who didn't know it was coming. Because I'm not sure which students knew and which students didn't, I am going to give you all a zero and you will have to make it up with an extra assignment." She gave the class a crooked grin before walking around her desk and taking her seat. "Let that be a lesson to all of you that cheating hurts everybody."

The class groaned and I cringed as several people shot me dirty looks.

"The assignment is on the board. It's a little ahead of

where we are, but I think we can get a lot out of it," Ms. Fisher continued. "Due tomorrow."

Everyone looked at the board. Write a one thousand word essay on how Richard Nixon's cheating affected our nation.

The class groaned again and Rachel squeezed my shoulder in silent support. I glanced over at Miller, but he kept his head buried in his history book. From what I could tell, he didn't look up the entire class.

Five minutes before the lunch bell was to ring, I packed up my stuff. I had to get to Miller before he disappeared down the hall. I had to talk to him. Or at least try.

I practically sprinted out of the room when the bell finally rang.

I grabbed his arm as he passed me. "We need to talk."

He shrugged me off. "I think you've done enough talking."

How could I make him understand? "Wait, Miller—that part's not true. You have to believe me."

Miller stopped in the hall, his face tight and hurt. "I kept wondering why you were hanging around me. Now I know. I thought you were different, but you're no better than those stuck-up snobs you hang out with."

Tears sprang up into my eyes. "Miller, you know me. Better than anyone. And you're the one who warned me about Sonya."

He gave me a long look. He wanted to believe me—I could see it in his eyes. "Is everything in it lies?"

I hesitated. "Well, not everything. Some of it is true. I was reading people's lips and telling my friends. But not that last thing about us. Sonya made that up." I looked at him pleadingly. "You have to believe me."

The disgust on his face twisted my heart.

"Why? Why should I believe someone who peeped in on people's private conversations and then told all of her friends so they could laugh about them?"

I stared at him, my eyes wide. Why should he?

He turned on his heel and walked off, his shoulders ramrod straight.

"Because I love you," I whispered as he disappeared among the other students.

I didn't want to go to lunch. I knew I couldn't eat anything. But Patrice and Rachel and the other girls would be waiting. They were sticking by me and I didn't want to let them down.

They sat at the usual table, and I remembered how I'd felt walking up to that table for the first time. Nervous, excited, scared. So much had happened since then. The friendships I'd made, my work at the kennels. Miller. Not to mention the feud with Sonya. The reason I could lose everything.

Patrice scooted over so I could sit between her and Rachel. "How's it going?"

I shrugged. "Miller won't talk to me. Everyone got an F

in American history thanks to me, and, oh, I might have ruined some teachers' lives. It's been better."

Patrice looked at me, her green eyes sympathetic. "If it helps, we have a meeting after the initiation stuff tonight."

Rachel, Kelly, Kayla, and I exchanged glances. Patrice must have caught it.

"What?" she demanded. "What's going on?"

But just then a hand clamped down onto my shoulder, causing me to jump, and the table went silent. I looked up to see Mr. Lutz standing over me.

"Miss Nelson, your presence is required in the office," he said.

The girls at the table froze.

"Okay." I stood up and followed Mr. Lutz, my heart pounding. *Here it comes.*

I avoided Mrs. Watson's disappointed gaze.

"Have a seat, young lady," Mr. Lutz said, leading me into his office. Mrs. Chandler, one of the counselors, was already there and sitting in one of the chairs.

He waited till I had settled into my chair before clearing his throat. "Mrs. Chandler is here as a witness. I take it you know why you are here."

I nodded.

"And even if I don't speak loudly enough, you can read my lips, correct?"

I nodded again.

He handed me a flyer. "Have you seen this?"

I bit my lip. "Yes, sir."

He leaned back in his chair in silence. I looked around the office, noting the ugly mustard carpeting and seventies-style furniture. Who would choose mustard-colored carpeting?

"Did you hand these out?"

His question brought me back to the conversation. I was about to get kicked out of school. *Focus.*

I shook my head. "No, sir."

He looked surprised. "Did you know what was on them before they were handed out?"

"I knew about the items on them, but I didn't know they would be printed and handed out around school."

"Are you this 'Scandal Diva'?"

I squirmed. How to answer that? "I guess so."

"I think you need to explain yourself a little better, Miss Nelson. You are in serious trouble."

I gulped and glanced at Mrs. Chandler, who gave me an encouraging smile. "I meant, I guess I am the Scandal Diva because I'm the one who found out all that stuff. But I never called myself the Scandal Diva and I never told anyone except a few people."

"Who told a few people, who told a few people?" Mr. Lutz's eyebrows met together in a scowl. I didn't blame him, considering.

"I guess so."

"How did you come by this information? I personally

know that none of these teachers would have said anything if they had known a student was around."

I looked at the ground. "I read their lips." I looked back up at him. "I read your lips."

He nodded, but Mrs. Chandler leaned forward.

"That's amazing," she said. "I've done some research on this, and most people get only about half of a conversation. Have you ever been tested? What is your accuracy rate?"

"I think it's like eighty-five percent."

Mrs. Chandler raised her eyebrows. "That's exceptional!"

Mr. Lutz cleared his throat and the counselor sat back in her seat.

"So you lip-read every one of these conversations?"

I nodded.

"Do you know what kind of trouble you've caused? Especially for our music and PE teachers? They came to me a little while ago with their resignation papers. I told them to hold on to them for now, but you may have ruined the careers of two excellent teachers."

"I don't think that's fair." Mrs. Chandler came to my defense. "They're adults. What they do on their own time is their business, but they were discussing the matter in the school. They brought it here. Serena only discovered it. In fact"—here she arched her eyebrows at Mr. Lutz— "I'd say that all the behavior listed here was brought about by people's own bad choices, except for the teacher whose pop quiz was ruined."

Mr. Lutz nodded, but his tight lips told me that I was still in big trouble.

He indicated the flyer. "And by handing these out, you told many people about it."

"No, I already told you I didn't do that. Why would I do that?" I pointed to the last item on the list. "I'm the new girl. Why would I hurt Miller? He's my friend. I wouldn't do that."

"A student came forward and said that you did."

My stomach turned. Three guesses as to who that was, and the first two didn't count.

"It was Sonya, wasn't it?" I asked.

"I'm not at liberty to say."

"She hates me. She said she was going to hurt me and she did." I paused and took a deep breath. "I'm really sorry those people got hurt. I know what I did was wrong, but I didn't set out to hurt anybody."

"So why *did* you do it?" Mrs. Chandler asked.

I looked at the floor. I couldn't tell them about the sorority. I was going to have to take the heat for this all on my own. "Because I wanted to fit in. I wanted people to like me."

Mrs. Chandler nodded as if she'd just had her suspicions confirmed.

Mr. Lutz picked up the phone. "At any rate, I'm calling your parents to come and get you. I'm going to have a meeting this evening with the counselors, and we will let you know what disciplinary measures will be taken. We may not have a policy against spreading gossip, but we do have a policy for stealing hall passes. Or stealing of any kind."

My throat closed and I widened my eyes to keep the tears from spilling over. My parents were going to be so disappointed in me. But not half as disappointed as I was in myself.

Fifteen

No one said a word on the drive home. Mom's face had whitened when the dean told her that I faced possible suspension. I had noticed Dad reach out to squeeze Mom's hand.

When we got home, I flopped down onto the couch to face the parentals. This day just kept getting better and better.

I waited for my parents to finish reading the flyer.

Dad raised his eyebrows. "The PE teacher got the music teacher pregnant? What kind of school do you go to?"

I shrugged.

Mom frowned at the paper and then looked at me. "Why don't you tell me how this started?"

I pulled the afghan off the back of the couch and wrapped it around my shoulders. "Everyone found out I could read lips and we thought we could have fun with it."

Dad waved at the paper. "And this is the stuff you found out?"

I nodded.

"What about this last item? I assume this is about Miller," Dad asked.

Tears welled up in my eyes. "That's a lie. I'd never do that. He doesn't believe me, though."

Silence.

Mom took a deep breath. "I take it you aren't the one who wrote this and handed it out, then?"

I shook my head.

Mom scowled. "Do you know who would?"

"A chick named Sonya. She's mad because I found her and Patrice's boyfriend making out at the party and then I told Patrice. She seriously didn't want me to be a part of the sorority."

Dad rolled his eyes. "So because of that, she hurt all these people?"

"She's not a very nice person."

"I guess not."

Mom stood up and paced around the room. "Why? Why did you do all this? Didn't you know it was wrong?"

Suddenly I was furious. And my parents just happened to be handy. "Because I wanted friends. Because you wanted me to have friends. The whole reason we moved here was so I could have friends. Well, I got 'em!"

I knew I was yelling but couldn't help it. The whole day

crashed on me and I couldn't take it anymore.

"I just wanted to fit in! Do you know how hard it is? No, you don't. You can't possibly know how hard it is for me!"

Okay, I sounded sorry for myself. I *was* sorry for myself. Why couldn't everyone just leave me alone? I hadn't wanted this. I ignored the little voice inside that said I *had* wanted this, that I had wanted to be in the sorority so much that I had been willing to risk everything for it.

I squirmed under Mom's level glare. "Stop feeling sorry for yourself. I didn't raise you that way. And from what I can tell, you caused a lot of this yourself."

She was right.

"Look, I'm sorry," I finally said. "This isn't your fault. It's mine because I knew I shouldn't have done it."

Dad shook his head. "I still can't believe the music teacher and the PE teacher were . . ."

Mom threw him a dirty look and he shrugged. I giggled through my tears. Geez. I couldn't seem to turn off the waterworks.

"I'm not sure what to do here. . . ." Mom trailed off.

"You can punish me if you want," I told her. "But I have to go to Jerry's this afternoon. It's really important."

"I think you can just forget about that—" Mom started, but Dad interrupted her.

"Very important?" he asked.

I nodded. "Yeah, it might help get me out of this mess." I raised my hand at the grim set of Mom's mouth. "Not that

I don't want to take responsibility for what I've done, but it might help me prove that I wasn't in this alone."

I held my breath. Dad finally nodded. "Fine. You can go to Jerry's, but you're not going anywhere afterward, so make up your mind to it. At least not until we find out what the school is going to do."

I jumped up and gave him a hug. "Thanks, Dad." I hugged my mom. "I'm sorry," I whispered. Then I ran upstairs. This had to work. It just had to.

I flopped down onto my bed and started counting. Mom came in by the time I hit fifty. Took her longer than I had thought. She didn't look angry, just very sad. She sat next to me.

She sniffled. "Your dad and I were talking. I know you call me the mother hover. I've known for a long time."

I tried to interrupt but she shushed me. "No, it's okay. I want you to be independent and I'm afraid of it at the same time. Afraid the world will knock you around. Well, it will, and it'll be worse because you're deaf. But the teen years aren't easy, and that's good because it means growth. I shouldn't shield you from that."

She was gonna make me cry again. "I wish you could have shielded me from this."

Her lips curved into a soft smile. "I'm going to try not to hover so much. To let you live your life, even if it means hard knocks. Everyone gets knocked around. Why should you be any different?"

Oh, great. I'd won the right to get hurt. Nice going. "I sort of like the mother hover. Makes me feel safe."

"Really?" Her eyes got all watery.

I giggled. "Kinda. You know what I mean."

Mom stood up and walked to the door.

"So does that mean we can talk about me getting my driver's license?" I asked.

Her skin turned ashen. "We can talk about it. Baby steps, hon. Baby steps."

I laughed as she went out the door.

Turning over on my bed, I thought about what she'd said. Without getting knocked around, you couldn't grow. If that was true, I should be growing like Jack's beanstalk right about now.

I glanced up at the drawing Miller had done for me and more tears pricked my eyes. I wanted to hide under the covers and forget about it, but something told me I wouldn't be forgetting about Miller for a long time. If ever. So I was going to have to be proactive. Take the bull by the horns or whatever cheesy cliché I wanted to use.

My phone flashed. It was Rachel.

Can U come to Jerry's? I can pick U up.

I typed back.

I'll B ready.

I checked myself out in the mirror. Oh, help! I wiped the makeup from around my eyes and put on some fresh eyeliner. I hesitated, then grabbed my black Volcom hoodie.

If I was going to have friends here, they'd have to take me the way I was. I left my pink T-shirt on underneath because, well, it was kinda cute.

I ran downstairs and out the door, just as Rachel pulled up.

I filled her in as we drove to Jerry's.

"So what are your parents going to do?" she asked on our way into the restaurant.

I shrugged. "Not sure. Depends on what the school does."

Suddenly I was surrounded by girls patting me on the back and giving me hugs. I choked up again. Gawd, I was turning into a regular fountain. We pulled some tables together to make one big one in the middle of the room.

"Has anyone seen any sorority girls?" Kayla asked, nibbling on some fries and keeping one eye on the door.

Mandy shook her head. "Not a one. Big stuff is going down. Though I'm sure they'll send someone to check up on us."

Just then Patrice slammed into the restaurant and marched toward us. The table went silent.

"Just what I need. On top of the day I've had, you all decide to freaking rebel!" She glared at us and then plopped down into an empty chair.

The day *she* had?

Rachel cleared her throat. "We just want to show everyone we are serious about standing by Serena."

The other girls nodded.

Patrice grabbed a mozzarella stick from Kelly. "You don't think I am? Gawd. I convinced Annie and Meredith to go to Mr. Lutz and tell him they had asked Serena to lip-read for them. I did, too."

"You did?" Waterworks time again.

Patrice nodded. "I got a big lecture on the privacy of others, blah blah blah. But the worst thing is that because our friend Sonya mentioned the sorority in the paper, we are now under attack. They're having a board meeting tomorrow night to decide what to do." She looked around at all of us. "So it doesn't matter if you all pull a coup. There may not be a sorority to belong to."

Silence descended on the table. Then all the girls babbled at once, and even though I couldn't hear all of them, I could tell how much the sorority meant to them. I had to do something, but what?

Wait, what was it Rachel had said yesterday? About how much power the alumnae had? Maybe they could help somehow.

I turned to Patrice. "I have an idea, but I need to talk to someone. Can you give me a lift up to my aunt's place?"

She nodded. "Sure. What kind of idea?"

I shook my head. "Not yet." I looked at the other girls. "Would you belong to the sorority if it was a bit different than what it is now, but still fun, with trips and stuff?"

Everybody nodded. I turned to Rachel. "I need a list of

the contact info for every former member you can think of. Can you e-mail that to me tonight?"

"No problem."

I stood up. "Ready?"

Patrice laughed. "I know this isn't funny, but I didn't expect you to morph into Super Serena."

I grinned at her. "And you haven't even seen my cape yet."

Patrice got me to the shelter in one piece, but I still wasn't sure how she had done it. Someone really needed to teach the girl how to drive.

My stomach tightened when I saw Miller's truck come into view. So he was here. I took a deep breath. *Have courage,* I told myself.

But first things first. I needed to talk to Aunt Shirley.

"Do you want me to stay?" Patrice asked.

I nodded. "Might as well. This affects you, too. Besides, I'm going to need your help." Patrice was a pro at manipulating adults. That might come in handy.

Aunt Shirley met us at the door. "What brings you two to my humble abode? Or should I even ask?"

I looked around the room.

"He's out in the kennels with the kids," she told me.

I nodded. "What have you heard?"

"All kinds of stuff. From the flyer Miller gave us, to a few hundred calls from concerned alumnae. I was actually going to get in touch with you today, so I'm glad you showed up." She indicated the living room and Patrice and I walked in. "Hi, Patrice. How's your mom?"

"She's fine. You should come visit sometime."

Aunt Shirley nodded. "I'll do that. Would you girls like something to drink or is this official sorority business?"

"Official business," I stated.

We sat on the old comfy couch and Aunt Shirley took the chair across from us.

"So what can I do for you?"

I took a deep breath and filled her in on what had happened. Patrice added what she knew.

"So what would you like me to do? You do have a plan, don't you?" She grinned at me. "I can see it all over you, Serena. Spill it."

"I do. I was wondering how we could get the school board to support the sorority, but I couldn't come up with anything. So, what if the sorority is taken outside the school and becomes like one of those clubs that's on its own?"

Understanding dawned on Patrice's face. "Like the Lions or the Garden Club or some other club like that, right?"

I nodded.

Aunt Shirley raised her eyebrows. "So, if the sorority exists outside the school they have no jurisdiction over it."

I took another deep breath. "Exactly. The sorority won't be allowed to exist as it is. We know that." I looked at Patrice. "But some changes will have to be made."

Aunt Shirley leaned forward and looked hard at Patrice. "How do you feel about that?"

Patrice thought for a moment, then shrugged. "I guess that would be okay, as long as I can still be president next year."

I giggled. Trust Patrice. But Aunt Shirley didn't even crack a smile—she just looked from me to Patrice as if judging us. The silence continued and even Patrice began to squirm.

Aunt Shirley finally relaxed, as if she'd made up her mind about something. "I have something to tell you, and I don't know how you're going to take it. The school administration isn't your only problem."

Patrice and I looked at each other. "What do you mean?" I asked.

"Some of the alumnae haven't been real pleased about the direction the sorority has taken the past few years. It's become more and more like a power trip for those in charge than a sisterhood and networking opportunity. They're thinking about shutting it down as well."

Patrice straightened. "They can't do that!"

"I assure you they can. Without the power of the alumnae helping one another out, what are the benefits?"

I watched as Patrice's face went white. "That isn't fair," she cried out. "Some of us have been waiting our whole life for this."

"Do you want it shut down?" I asked Aunt Shirley.

"That depends. What can you guys do to turn things around? Come up with a good plan and I'll talk to the other alumnae about it. No one wants to shut down a thirty-year tradition, but we're all adults now. None of us approve of the behavior exhibited by the current class of sorority members in the name of the sorority."

Patrice slumped in her seat and I cast her a sympathetic look. She must have been mortified to learn that the alumnae of a group she wanted to head up found her wanting.

Aunt Shirley stood and gave a small smile. "I'm going to go ahead and get you both something to drink and let you talk. Pulling the sorority out of the school is a good start. What else can you come up with?" she walked out of the room.

Patrice closed her eyes for a minute. "This is so bad, Serena. You don't even know. We have to think of something."

"Well, we've taken it out of the school to make it more like an active club. Maybe we can have a member of the alumnae supervise us?"

She glanced toward the doorway. "I don't want some stodgy old woman looking over our shoulders all the time. What fun is that?"

I shrugged. "So make it a college-age person. Someone who knows more about what it is to be a teenager."

"I can live with that. That might be pretty cool, actually. And bylaws. Adults love bylaws. So our first order of business in the new sorority is to come up with some bylaws."

"We could be less exclusive," I suggested. "They would probably love that."

Patrice shook her head. "Absolutely not. I refuse to be in a sorority that will let just anyone in. Girls should have to strive to belong."

"I agree with Patrice." Aunt Shirley came back into the room and handed us both a glass of iced tea. "The hallmark of the sorority has always been excellence. Though perhaps popularity shouldn't be the only mark of excellence you judge by." She set a plate of cookies down onto the coffee table and flashed us both a knowing grin.

Patrice outlined her plan and Aunt Shirley nodded. "That just might work," she said. "Now, what do you propose to do about the school board?"

"Use the power of alumnae," I said. "This is a small town. I bet almost everyone on that school board has someone in their family who was in the sorority."

"Genius!" Patrice breathed. "You're right!"

I grinned at Aunt Shirley. "Can you give me some names of some women who might support us? A little pull on the school board wouldn't hurt."

She laughed. "I take it you didn't know that I'm on the school board?"

My jaw dropped. She really was like the Godfather. "No! Are there any other alumnae on the board?"

"Not on the board, but Mrs. Watson was in the sorority. She takes the notes for the board meetings."

Would the surprises never end?

"Okay, that's just weird and a little bit creepy," Patrice said.

I agreed.

Aunt Shirley grinned and grabbed her address book. "Here," she said a few minutes later, handing me a piece of paper. "I think these women will be more than happy to help you."

I was quiet for a moment. "I have to fix this, Aunt Shirley."

She looked thoughtful, then nodded. "I'm in."

I sighed in relief and Patrice clapped. Now it was time to face Miller. "I need to go talk to someone. Will you be okay here?" I asked Patrice.

She nodded. "I need more sugar anyway," she said, snatching up another cookie.

I walked slowly out to the kennels, wondering what I was going to say. Or if he would even talk to me at all. My stomach, which I didn't think could take any more abuse, tied itself into knots and my feet dragged.

The boys mobbed me when I walked in. Miller had his back to me, but I could tell by the way he stiffened that he knew I was there. I hugged the boys, wondering when I had gotten so fond of their small grubbiness. I shooed them into the house, telling them that their mom had snacks for them. Aunt Shirley wouldn't let me down.

"You don't have to say anything," I told Miller's back. "Just hear me out, okay?"

He didn't turn, but I figured he was listening.

"I know what I did was wrong. I didn't mean for it to happen—it all just kind of got out of hand. But before you judge me, try to see my side. I've never belonged anywhere, and they offered me a chance to belong, to be a part of this very cool, exclusive club." I bit my lip, trying to figure out a way to get him to understand. "I really wanted to, even though I knew they were using me. But that didn't have anything to do with us. I just want you to know that I'm just . . ." I paused, feeling stupid. He hadn't even turned around. "I'm just sorry."

He didn't move and I felt my heart plunge. But I could only tell him the truth.

"Think about it, okay? I understand if you don't want to be with me, but I wanted you to know that." My voice choked and I ran out the door. I couldn't stand to see the anger and disappointment in his eyes if he ever turned around. Patrice was waiting by the car and she opened my door. "Are you ready?" she asked. Time to visit the alumnae and plead our case.

I nodded, got in, and sat back in my seat. I had done my best. With everything. Only time would tell if it was enough.

The next evening Patrice, Rachel, and I waited for the powers that be to decide the fate of the sorority. We were sitting outside the high school. The board meeting was taking place in about twenty minutes, and according to Rachel, the alumnae dinner meeting was already taking place at her house on the other side of town.

"What do you think is gonna happen?" Patrice asked for the gazillionth time.

I shook my head as Rachel shrugged. We'd done the best we could. After leaving Aunt Shirley's last night, Patrice and I had visited with several alumnae members, including Rachel's mom, a city-council member, and, oddly enough, Mrs. No-Butts Lutz herself. We explained our plan and left it in their hands. Actually, I let Patrice do most of the talking. She was so good at it. They would either support us or not at the dinner tonight.

Rachel's mom had kicked her out early. Only five women had arrived by the time she left and Rach had recognized a few of them.

I'd spent most of the day at home, reading and helping Mom work on her office. The word from the school had come. I got a three-day suspension for stealing hall passes and would no longer be allowed to work in the office. But it wouldn't go on my permanent record. The sentence was retroactive, so I'd be back in school on Monday.

A car drove up and Mr. Lutz and his wife got out. Then Aunt Shirley arrived with a woman I had never seen before.

Other cars began arriving. Mr. Lutz didn't look at us as he passed, but Mrs. Lutz gave us a quick smile. We hopped up from our seat on the front steps and moved to go inside.

Mr. Lutz barred our way. "Sorry, girls. It's a closed meeting."

Patrice shook her head decisively. "No, board meetings are public."

"Those are monthly board meetings. This is a special meeting and it's up to administration discretion. We decided a closed board meeting would be best."

Patrice stepped back, her mouth open. We couldn't even speak in our defense.

Aunt Shirley winked at us as she went by. We looked at one another.

"What now?" Rachel asked.

"We wait," Patrice told her.

"But why are we waiting here?" I asked. "The school board can't stop us from taking the sorority outside the school—it's the alumnae who can put a stop to everything. We should go hang out in front of Rachel's place."

"Good idea." Patrice grabbed her purse. "This bites."

Rachel shook her head, her blond hair swinging in negation. "Are you kidding me? I was threatened. I didn't know my mom could be that scary."

"We'll pull in down the street. She won't know that we're there," Patrice promised. "Besides, I hate feeling powerless."

We headed for her car. Just before we climbed in, Patrice tossed Rachel her phone. "I changed my mind. I want them to know we're there. Start texting every name that has an S in front of it. Tell them to meet us at your house. If the alumnae are going to shut us down, they're going to have to say it to our faces."

"Should I text Sonya?" Rachel asked.

Patrice nodded. "I have a thing or two to say to her."

She took off amid a squeal of tires and I prayed we'd make it there safely. No one said a word that I could tell on our way there. Rachel texted like a madwoman while Patrice was busy driving recklessly.

The sun was setting by the time we came to a stop in front of Rachel's. I wondered what Patrice's next move would be. I didn't have to wonder long when I spotted Meredith and Annie walking toward the car.

We hopped out and Meredith raised her eyebrows when she saw Rachel and me. "Patrice, we need to talk, but lose the initiates."

Patrice shook her head and slammed her door. "Nope, they stay. They have as much to lose as the rest of us, and Serena's aunt is helping us."

Meredith shrugged. "Fine, whatever. So what did you want to do here? Stage a protest? Don't you think the alumnae are going to shut us down or not as they choose?"

"Yeah, but a lot of these women are moms." Patrice smirked. "It'll be way harder to tell us something bad to our smiling, hopeful faces." Her eyes widened into a picture of innocent anticipation.

You had to hand it to her. No one could read and handle adults like Patrice. Really, the chick should go into politics.

"Couldn't hurt." Annie said. More cars were pulling up, and my heart swelled as the girls who had supported me came and stood next to Rachel and me. No matter what happened with the sorority, I now belonged in a way I never had before.

"Come on, let's go stand on the lawn so they can see us," Patrice called out.

About thirty-five girls walked over to Rachel's yard and began milling about, staring at the blinds that covered the front window. You could almost feel the tension.

"Watch the flowers," Rachel warned, and giggled nervously.

"What now?" I whispered to Kelly.

I didn't catch her reply. Hearing anything was out of the question because so many girls were whispering. All I got was an annoying hum, and I turned up my hearing aids to see if I could pick up anything.

Suddenly it all stopped. The blinds to Rachel's front picture window opened all the way. The women inside were brightly etched against the lights, which spilled out onto the lawn. They seemed to be having a wonderful time. I even saw a few look out at us and smile. Someone was passing out snacks on a tray and most of the women had drinks in their hands. Were they deliberating on the future of the sorority or having a party?

The front door opened and Rachel's mom stepped out, carrying a bright red drink in one hand. She flicked on a porch light, illuminating the front yard. "It's fine, girls. We're not going to kill the sorority. We like the new ideas you guys came up with and will be in touch with the president and the president-elect shortly to start implementing the changes. But for now, go away and let us enjoy ourselves!"

After a moment of stunned silence a loud shout rang out, and I winced before quickly turning my hearing aids back down. Kelly and Rachel wrapped me in a hug.

Patrice fought her way over to us and joined in the hug fest. "Let's all go to Jerry's," she said. "We have a lot of planning to do." She waved at Annie and Meredith, who were already heading back to their car.

"I'm in. I have no idea when this"—Rachel waved her arm toward the house, where the women inside still milled about eating and laughing—"is going to be over."

Patrice grabbed my arm. "I want you to be secretary next year, Serena."

I chuckled to myself. In spite of all the changes in Patrice, there were some things that she just didn't get. But that was okay. I did. "Thanks, but I can't. I'm deaf, Patrice. The secretary has to be able to listen to everyone at the same time and then take notes. I can't do that."

"Oh." Her face was troubled for a moment before clearing. "No worries. I have a job perfect for you."

I raised an eyebrow at her.

"You can be our spokesperson."

My heart stopped. "Our what?" I asked stupidly.

"I want you to be the person who represents our sorority to the press and at all the official meetings, and you can run fundraisers and stuff."

She wanted me to speak for the sorority? With my funny voice? I just nodded. Right then I couldn't have spoken if I had wanted to.

"I think it's perfect," Rachel said, and some of the other girls agreed.

We started to move toward our car but stopped short as Sonya appeared before us.

The snapping fury in her green eyes belied the mocking stillness of her face. "Congratulations, Patrice. You're now the president of a loser sorority."

Patrice's eyes ran up and down Sonya coolly. "I'd say you were the loser, Sonya. Not only are you the class leper, but Scott doesn't want anything to do with you."

That was news to me.

Sonya's lip curled. "Like I'd want him. *I've* already had him. Besides, I'm still class secretary and head cheerleader. You can't change that."

Patrice gave Sonya a level look, her eyes icy. "Don't get used to it. When I'm through with you, you'll be lucky to get elected to take out the garbage."

Sonya tossed her hair. "That's what you think." She

looked at the girls I had thought of as Sonya-ites. "Come on, Kayla, Mandy—let's get out of here."

No one moved. A panicked look crossed Sonya's face.

Kayla linked her arms with her sister. "I'm gonna hang out with Patrice and Kel tonight."

Mandy stared hard at the grass and didn't budge.

Sonya bit her lip.

Not so confident now, are ya, Sonar?

Patrice smirked. "Next year you'll be begging me to get into the sorority."

"Fat chance," Sonya hissed.

"Sonya!" A woman's voice rang out behind me and we all turned.

A pretty, dark-haired college-age girl stalked up to us and stood facing Sonya with her hands on her hips.

Sonya's eyes widened and she backed up a step. "Christina, what are you doing home from school?"

"I drove home when I got the summons that the sorority was in trouble. How surprised was I to find out that it was my little sister who'd sold us out?"

"No, I didn't mean for that to happen. I—"

Christina cut her off. "We'll talk about it at home."

When Sonya opened her mouth again, Christina pointed toward the cars. "Go." Sonya went.

Then Christina looked at Patrice and smiled. "I hear you'll be president next year. Congrats. I'm going to be your adult adviser."

Patrice squealed. "That's fabulous. I'm glad it's you. I thought they were going to give us Mrs. Watson or something!"

Christina grinned and shook Patrice's hand. "It'll be fun. I'll be in touch."

Christina took off toward her car.

"I think someone's going to be in trouble." Patrice commented watching them disappear into the darkness. The streetlights flicked on. "Her sister will probably want her in the sorority, though. Whatever—we'll just make Sonya pay for the next couple of weeks and then welcome her back with open arms. That'll teach her to mess with people's lives." She winked at me and I laughed. "Anyone need a ride?" Patrice asked.

"I do," I said.

"No, she's going with me," a voice said loudly from my left.

My breath caught as Miller emerged from the shadows. Patrice and the others grinned and drifted away. Soon we were alone.

"Come over here," he said, taking my arm.

Tingles ran over my skin as they always did when he touched me. "Where are we going?"

"Here," he said, stopping under a streetlamp. "I want to make sure you get everything I have to say."

"Who told you where I was?"

"A little birdie named Shirley. Now quiet. I have something to say."

I waited, hope thrumming through my body along with the electricity from his hands, now holding mine. His lean face, lit up by the light, had never looked so good.

"I thought about what you said and you're right. I don't know what it's like to be you. Just like you don't know what it's like to be me." He paused and took a deep breath. "I think that's why we've had so much trouble with each other. We're both clumsy like that. Neither one of us can get out of our own head long enough to see the other's point of view. And I want to say I'm sorry."

I tried to protest, but he dropped my hand and put his finger against my lips. "I'm sorry that I didn't listen to you. I'm sorry I didn't believe you. Serena . . . I love you."

My heart soared as I read his lips. I heard him loud and clear.

Teri Brown has been working as a free-lance writer for the past eight years. She is a contributing editor for iParenting Media and the author of two published nonfiction books on homeschooling and field trips. Her magazine credits include *Writer's Digest, Women's Health & Fitness, Dog Fancy, Oregon Coast,* and *Road King,* among many others. When not writing, taking care of her animals, or dealing with the jungle that is her Portland, Oregon, backyard, she hangs out with her two teenagers, her deaf teenage niece, and all their various and sundry friends. This is her first young adult novel. You can visit her on the Web at www.teribrownwrites.com.

Girls searching for answers . . .
and finding themselves.

Lauren Baratz-Logsted   Anita Liberty   Cheryl Diamond

Teri Brown   Blake Nelson

From Simon Pulse | Published by Simon & Schuster

Get ready
for the newest
Private novel:

AMBITION

Now Available

And don't miss the first six books in the Private series:

From bestselling author
KATE BRIAN

♥ ♥ ♥ ♥ ♥

Juicy reads for the sweet and the sassy!

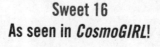

Sweet 16
As seen in *CosmoGIRL!*

Lucky T
"Fans of Meg Cabot's *The Princess Diaries* will enjoy it." —*SLJ*

Megan Meade's Guide to the McGowan Boys
Featured in *Teen* magazine!

The Virginity Club
"*Sex and the City: High School Edition.*" —*KLIATT*

The Princess & the Pauper
"Truly exceptional chick-lit." —*Kirkus Reviews*

FROM SIMON PULSE
♥ Published by Simon & Schuster ♥

Looking for something quirky and fun?

~~~ Kristen Tracy ~~~

Praise for *Lost It*:

★ "Readers will fall in love with this offbeat story."
—*Publisher's Weekly*, starred review

"Full of hilarious dialogue...." —*VOYA*

~~~ From Simon Pulse | Published by Simon & Schuster ~~~